I0682748

WANTED UNDEAD OR ALIVE

RENEE JOINER

OSHUN
PUBLICATIONS
oshunpublications.com

The Vengeful and the Vindicated

Venture into the shadowy realm of personal retribution, where the line between hunter and hunted becomes blurred.

Half Demon

Wanted Undead or Alive

Witch's Justice

Ancestor's Magic

Red Rising

THERE ARE ALSO AUDIOBOOKS!

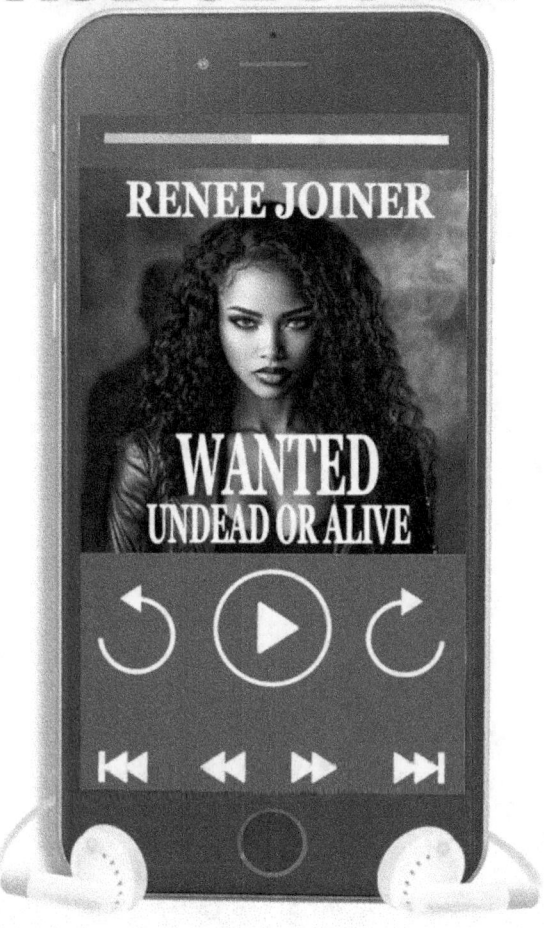

reneejoinerauthor.com/audiobooks

JOIN MY
NEWSLETTER

GET UPDATES,
FREEBIES & GIVEAWAYS

RENEEJOINERAUTHOR.COM/NEWSLETTER

ONE

Amirah

_____

AMIRAH RUBBED HER TEMPLES AND CLOSED HER EYES AS she listened to the woman on the other end of the phone. Usually, the beautiful view from her office, took the edge of the frustration she felt for her clients at times. Today, however, she felt unsettled, and not even her beautiful view could settle this feeling churning inside of her.

"All I am saying, Kayla, is that you do not need a man to define who you are," Amirah sighed. Some women were definitely born out of time. "This is the twenty-first century; women need to be more assertive."

Amirah shook her head as she listened to Kayla Craft, one of the city's most well-known socialites, needing a strong dominant male in her life. Kayla had the power to lead women to empower themselves and be their own driving force. Although she was a well-known figure whom men desired, and women wanted to be, that was only her social face. According to the world, Kayla had it all: fame, power, and men falling over themselves for her. Behind the scenes, Kayla was a lonely, desperate, lost soul wanting to be nurtured, pampered, taken care of, but mostly dominated. Amirah slipped into her plush leather chair, glancing once again over Kayla's ideal partner profile. It really was true that people were different creatures behind closed doors.

"Kayla, I know you want to keep a low profile about this, but come to the social mixer on Saturday night," Amirah made a note on a pad to get her assistant, Rachel, to send tickets to Kayla. "I will introduce you as a close personal friend, so no one will know you joined a dating service." On the same note, Amirah jotted down a few male client names for Rachel to invite that may suit Kayla's requirements. "I will see you at seven on Saturday," she listened to Kayla's misgivings. "Of course, I will get Rachel to keep an eye out for you," Amirah hung up. She had never had a headache in her life, but she was sure if she had to speak to Kayla for another few minutes, she would have had her first.

"Rachel," Amirah walked through to her assistant's adjoining office. "I need you to send a few tickets for Saturday night's mixer to Kayla Ambrose," she put the note on Rachel's desk. "Also, can you make sure that the men listed here are attending? I think there may be a few that Kayla would enjoy."

Amirah's eyebrows rose up at the expression on her assistance face. "What?" she looked down at the list. "You don't think those men would be a good match?"

"No," Rachel took the note and Kayla's file. "I just think that you need to realize that not all women are like you." Rachel looked at her boss; she was beautiful, confident, and empowering, but at the same time, very intimidating. "Not all women can or want to have to take the initiative or be in the driving seat all the time,"

Rachel leaned over to grab a pile of folders on her desk, which she placed in front of Amirah. "These are the four clients we have lost in the past two weeks who don't want to be empowered."

"So, what are you saying?" Amirah spread the folders, noting the names of two of her most prominent clients that had been with her for almost a year. "That I don't at least try and help these women?" She picked up the files. "That I should just let them go through life, allowing men to run roughshod all over them?"

"No, Amirah," Rachel knew Amirah's secret, yet she was not afraid of her. In fact, she loved Amirah, who had become like a sister to her and had saved her life. "I am saying that maybe just ease up a little and let your clients have their own opinions and taste in men." Rachel placed Amirah's favorite latte laced with a bit of O-negative in front of her, "Here you go, one Virgin Mary Latte."

Amirah breathed in the scent of fresh O-neg mixed with the heady aroma of her favorite coffee beans roasted to perfection by Rachel. "Nice save," Amirah shook her head at her cheeky assistant and ambled back into her office, pondering what Rachel had said. Maybe the girl was right; perhaps she did need to ease up a bit on her clients. After all, Amirah ran the most prominent and elite dating agency in the country that prided itself on finding their clients the perfect match. How could she promise that when she was, in fact, probably trying to match all the women with her perfect match?

That is when it hit her; it had been way too long since she had a reasonable date, let alone anything else. She looked at her slim gold wristwatch. It was time to call it a day. Besides, she could do with a new pair of shoes and a matching purse. She looked down at the elegant heels she had on. Maybe red; she liked burgundy, but that was last week's color.

"Good night, Rachel," Amirah breezed past her assistant, not wanting to get the third degree about her plans or that maybe she needed a good night out from the girl. "Be a good girl and lock up for me." She smiled as she stepped into her elevator that only serviced her floor. It was basically always waiting for her when she needed it.

Before Rachel had time to respond, the doors slid shut, and the elevator started its descent to the ground floor. As it went down, Amirah felt a bit frustrated by the events of the day. Yes, maybe she should not try and force her women's empowerment agenda on her clients. But a lot of the women who lived in this day and age did not know how fortunate they were. Amirah had often wanted to be able to let them know just how damn lucky they were. She could tell them horrible tales of being a fourteen-year-old girl in the sixteenth century.

~ ~ ~

As Amirah browsed the store for a leather handbag to match her new pair of handmade Italian pumps, her keen senses once again picked up a scent. It was the same one that had been on her tail since she had left her office. Granted, it was subtle and really well masked; making her think that whoever it was that was following her was a pro. In fact, she had actually considered at one stage during her shopping spree she imagined it. She probably would not have picked up the scent at all, except this one was very distinct.

Her hair prickled at the back of her neck; she felt decidedly uneasy, a feeling she had not felt since… She shuddered, squashing the urge to take a trip down that particular memory lane. There was only one thing to do here, and that was to slip her shadow. Not giving away that she knew she was being followed, Amirah continued wondering about the shopping center, browsing the shop windows. She even popped into a few for good measure before stopping at a mobile coffee shop and getting a latte before making her way to the ladies. She sighed as she ducked into the end stall by the window and slipped off her burgundy heels. Not that they would have hindered her escape, but she did not feel like ruining her favorite shoes. She tested the window, which was sealed shut, but it was no problem for her. With a thump, it popped right open. She skillfully edged her way through it and ducked over the rooftops to her apartment with her tail still waiting back in the mall.

~ ~ ~

Amirah placed a warm relaxing mask over her amber eyes and lay back on her couch with a glass of Merlot next to her. She took a deep breath and willed her long, lithe subtle body to relax. She never really needed to sleep, but scaling buildings did take a bit more effort, not to mention what the stress of not being seen did to a vampire. She also needed to think about the events of the day. Such as rethinking her work strategy, and why she was being followed. Or, more importantly, who was following her. If it was an amateur, Amirah would have laughed it off; she may have played a few games with whomever. She had come across her equal share of amateur hunters, wronged by her kind and out for revenge. Not that Amirah wronged humans in any way; she had her moral code by which she lived, thanks to her vampire family. But this, this was a professional, which could mean only one of two things. Before she could ponder over it more, her doorbell chimed.

Amirah knew who was there before she had sat up on the couch. It was Morgan, one of her sires. She wondered was why Morgan had suddenly turned up on her doorstep when he had called her from Amsterdam not more than forty-eight hours ago.

"Morgan, this is a …," as Amirah swung the door to her apartment open, she could smell his wound even before he collapsed into her arms, dragging them to the floor. "What in the world?" Her eyes scanned his long torso looking for the wound only to find blood seeping from his ears. "Morgan!" Amirah shook his face, "Honey, what happened?" she gently pushed him off her and started to stand when he pulled her back down towards him.

"Saa…" he tried to croak, swallowing profusely like he was trying to wet a dry mouth or throat. "S s s…" Before he could speak again, his eyes flew open wide like he had been shocked.

"Morgan, what is it?" Amirah put her hand under his head, and, as she put her hand on his chest, it disintegrated into ash that filtered through her fingers like sooty sand.

TWO

Luka

LUKA BROCK KNEW HOW TO KEEP HIS DISTANCE. HE HAD been in covert operations for a very long time. Luka was also one, if not the best in his line of work. At least he had been before half his elite team ended up being ripped apart in an operation that had gone horribly wrong. Images of that mission still haunted his dreams when he actually managed to get in an hour or two of sleep at night. He gave himself a mental shake as the screams and terrible sounds of breaking bones echoed through his head. Now was not the time for a bout of PTSD, or what his mandatory shrink called his night terrors and freezing in mid-operation. He called it wimping out and losing his nerve. Luka artfully stepped up to the donut shop and ordered a pretzel because it did not carry as much scent as his favorite caramel-glazed donut. From the corner of his eye, he could see his charge turn around and glance over the crowd uneasily.

"Yup," he muttered, leisurely taking a bite of the pretzel, as he blended in with the evening rush in the busy mall. "The charge knows I'm here." Luka wiped his mouth to hide that he was talking to himself. Well, he was not really talking to himself but into a very well-concealed state-of-the-art communication system. One designed so no supernatural creature with super sensitive hearing would pick up.

"Losing your touch there, old man," the voice of his sassy assistant and partner in training, although she still pretty much only did office duty, came through the comms device.

"Watch it there, missy. Remember, I know all the instructors at the academy where you will be taking your field exams in less than ..." he took another bite of his pretzel, really wishing it was a donut.

"Three weeks, twelve hours, and twenty minutes to be exact, and as you well know!" Sophie huffed. "You could always buy me a nice watch to throw the charge off."

"What?" he was so busy watching one of the most gracefully beautiful women he had ever seen trying on a pair of high heels. He lost track of the conversation he was having with his earpiece.

"A watch!" Sophie elaborated. "You know, those things that help you tell time and something that maybe you should actually invest in for yourself?"

Confused, he noticed he was actually standing at the watch counter. He looked around, seeing three security cameras all focused in his direction. "Really, Soph?" Luka shook his head at her. "These cameras are for store security, not for playing peeping Tom on me."

"Ask for a watch," Sophie told him. "Your charge is heading towards the register to pay for those really ridiculously priced leather items she is buying. Do people ever even think of the animals that had to die for them?"

"A little green there, honey?" he drawled, a rare smile splitting his handsome face.

"Excuse me, sir?" the tall skinny man, who looked a lot like Riff Raff from the Rocky Horror Show, asked him.

"Uh… nothing. Sorry, I was just thinking how jealous this watch would make my wife's friends," he smiled at the shop assistant, making the man blush and almost swoon. Luka was a ruggedly handsome man complete with a chiseled profile, thick dark hair, and deep blue eyes. When he bestowed a rare smile, it added to his raw sex appeal.

"It would complement any woman," the flustered assistant managed to stammer out.

"Nice save there, Tarzan. I think you made his whole day, even if you were too cheap to buy a watch," Sophie laughed just as his phone beeped, indicating a message.

He pulled it out once again, shaking his head as a picture of the shop assistant fanning himself from Luka's smile appeared on his screen. "Seriously, Soph?"

"Well, you get to have all the fun in the field," she told him before alerting him to the fact that his charge had just left the store.

"Which way?" he took his time browsing through some wallets.

"Turn left out the store door and then head into the lingerie shop," she laughed again. "Are you blushing?"

"Are you still playing with the store's surveillance cameras?" he countered, a little embarrassed about his awkwardness around shops that only stocked women's underwear. In fact, he did not even like saying the word lingerie, but for some reason, his assignments always seemed to land him up in or close to one. What was wrong with the people in the medical profession to which he usually got assigned? They seemed obsessed with lacy undergarments? Okay, so the underwear they bought was not all lacy. Some of the things he had watched them buy he could, unfortunately, never unsee. This time, he was assigned a charge that was not in the medical profession, and somehow on the very first day, he lands right back at a lingerie shop.

"I would say touché, but I am just enjoying those lovely rosy cheeks you have there, boss!" she laughed, making the store camera move up and down like it was laughing too.

Luka walked casually along, looking into the shop windows, checking his texts while he walked. Or at least, that is how he appeared to everyone around him; he was, in fact, keeping a watchful eye on his charge. He ignored Sophie's sarcastic teasing as his instincts tingled, a warning sign he once trusted without any doubt. These days, not so much; he dealt with things he could see, facts that were hard to dispute, and hard evidence to back up those facts. Still, he did acknowledge his instincts. He just no longer followed them blindly, and right now, they were going from tingling to a full-blown banshee scream. His skin prickled as goose flesh marched up along his arms, and he knew without a shadow of a doubt he was being watched. He turned to make it look like he was looking for someone, glancing at his watch for added effect as he expertly scanned the shopping mall crowd.

"Your charge went to the restrooms," Alison

informed him, obviously seeing him craning his neck and mistaking the gesture as him looking to see which way they had gone. "That shop really has you turned around there."

Sophie was having way too much fun with his discomfort; in fact, she had been acting weird since they had taken on their new charge. Or maybe it was her looming field exams that had her sarcasm and pranks reaching new levels in the control room as of late.

"Ah, got it, thanks," Luka played along with her, not wanting to alert her that he now knew he was being watched. He saw the culprit quickly duck away into the crowd and disappear. Well, that could not be good. He glanced at his watch; no one took this long in the bathroom. His eyes scoured the building; yup, his charge had done a runner and was probably skipping across the rooftops right about now.

"So, you lost her," Sophie sighed. "The great Luka Brock got the shake off," her laughter echoed through his headpiece.

~ ~ ~

"How long are you going to carry on about this?" Luka asked. He supposed he could tell her that he was about to let Amirah give him the slip as he felt she knew she was being tailed. He could also tell her that he was being tailed, but he did not want to put any of them in danger until he found out why. But instead, he let her have her fun, at least, for now, that is.

"I may be an absolute legend at what I do," he finished his last chin up; his body gleamed with sweat from his work out. "I may also be in peak shape," he dried himself off with a towel, after which he scrunched it into a ball and threw it into the corner basket. "But my dear Sophie, I, unlike our lady vamp across the way there," he pointed, knowing that Sophie could see everything he saw through his new spy wear glasses, "cannot leap tall buildings in a few bounds."

"Single bound," Sophie corrected. "If you are going to quote Superman, make sure you do it right."

"Oh, I know it was single bound, but I doubt even our remarkable lady vamp across the way can fly." He stared into the luxurious apartment across the way from where his company had installed him.

"Okay, I will give you that one, and you are right; nothing in her file says she can fly," Sophie confirmed. "That would have been cool, though."

"Nerd," he teased her. "I see she has wandered off into the for-your-eyes-only zone." Luka checked the recording devices to make sure they were all on and set. He had listening devices and cameras set up in Amirah's apartment, but one never knew when they needed a backup. "I am going to take a quick shower while you keep an eye on the charge."

Luka pulled a bottle of water from the fridge and popped a TV dinner into the microwave before settling down to watch The Amirah Show. Before he could take a bite of his dinner, the doorbell rang. His hand slid beneath the cushion of the couch and pulled out his gun. He checked it and silently crept to the door, snatching up the telescopic glasses, he switched them to x-ray vision. The glasses expertly assessed his visitor, informing him it was an agent of the Paranormal Supervision and Investigation agency. Hiding the weapon in the back of his jeans, Luka opened the door to greet one of his partners, Jeff Daniels.

"I see they gave you the new spy gear toys to play with," Jeff checked out the glasses. "Cool. What are they like?"

"Quite awesome actually," Luka pulled the glasses off and put them on the counter. "So, what brings you by, Jeff?"

"Can't I visit my partner?" Jeff's boyish face looked all innocent.

"Sure," Luka shrugged before heading back to his TV dinner. "I would offer, but this is all I cooked."

"Hell, no. I would not touch that stuff if you paid me to." Jeff looked on in disgust at the meal Luka was about to poison his system with. "Actually, the firm asked me to pop by and see that you had everything you need; you know, see if all the equipment was here, that sort of thing."

"You mean to check up on me to see that I am not blowing my first civilian undercover mission in two years?" Luka raised his eyebrow at Jeff.

"Well, maybe and ... hey, is that..." Jeff's attention was caught by the beauty gliding across her living room floor to her kitchen. Her long lithe body covered in a blue kimono, her long dark hair floated in thick waves down her back. She was mesmerizing; both men stared at the screen, captivated by how she moved, only to be rudely brought back to life by a harrumph from Luka's earpiece.

"Are you bozos gawking?" Sophie raised her voice,

blasting Luka's eardrum. "What is wrong with you both?"

"Sophie?" Jeff, who was sitting beside Luka, pointed to his ear. He could hear her every word; she was so loud. Luka nodded in confirmation before switching off the TV. "They assigned you, Amirah?" Jeff looked at him, confused, laced with a bit of annoyance.

"Yeah," Luka looked at him, frowning. "Why do you sound so surprised?"

"Do you know who she is?" Jeff looked at Luka with something that actually looked a bit like concern.

"Yes, I have all the intel on her," Luka watched as Jeff looked at the file on the table, flipping through it without asking, before Luka took it back. "Do you mind? That is classified information. Geez, Jeff, you know the rules, man."

"No, buddy, each day that goes by, I have to wonder about the rules," Jeff stood up and walked towards the front door, stopping as he pulled it open to say, "Nothing about being assigned by a high-profile vampire charge like Amirah made you ask why they did?"

"No, actually, now that I think about it, I did wonder why they had chosen me when she is no longer my MO," he had followed Jeff to the door; the two guys looked worried, each for their own reasons.

"Well, I am going to do a bit of digging," Jeff's voice dropped. He indicated towards Luka's ear, and then used sign language to let him know he did NOT have all the information on Amirah. He also said he would be in touch soon, then left.

There was that feeling again; his instincts starting to do their niggling. Surely Jeff was being overdramatic and cautious here. Luka had everything under control, and from what he had seen, Amirah was not that dangerous. She lived within the rules, and as far as he could tell, she actually made a point of trying to help humans.

As he wandered back into the room, Sophie warned him that Amirah had a visitor; her doorbell had just rung. In his hurry to see who it was, Luka grabbed the glasses, not noticing the small blue light that silently clicked off before he put them back on.

Luka watched Amirah sit up on her couch and pull her mask off before padding over to her front door. A vampire fell through the door, toppling him and Amirah to the ground. She raised her hand, and Luka could see it was covered in blood.

"Do we know who her visitor is?" Luka asked Sophie, and then said, "Holy hell, what just happened?" Both he and Sophie watched from their vantage point as the giant of a vampire turned into what, at first, seemed like nothing but dust.

THREE

Hunting a Hunter

AMIRAH PACED HER LIVING ROOM, GLANCING AT HER watch every few minutes. What the hell had happened to Morgan? She had never seen anything like that in all the years she had been on earth, and she had been on earth for a very long time. She knew of a few things that could instantly kill a vampire but nothing that would turn them into dust, or rather, ash. All these years, she had laughed at the silly vampire movies and how they stereo-typed them for not being able to go out in the sun. Sure, they had super sensitive skins, and the sun made them sick; yes, it could probably kill them, but it can kill humans too. Where humans got skin cancer, if vampires did not take extra precautions in the sun, they got an accelerated type of skin cancer. It would eat through their skin like necrotizing fasciitis—a flesh-eating disease—did. What sun exposure did not do was make vampires crumble into ash. Neither did a wooden or silver stake through the heart; yes, it killed them, but a stake through anyone's or any creature's heart would kill them. Whereas a vampire could heal from just about any injury, the two things they could not come back from was being beheaded or staked through the heart.

Something that niggled at Amirah was what the weird smell in Morgan's blood was. Vampires could pick up on the minutest of changes in any creature's blood, but with Morgan, she did not pick up any foreign bodies in his blood. Yet, the smell of his blood was off, like it was rotting. Now she wished she had had time to gather some of his blood to get it analyzed.

She needed answers and was convinced she would get her answers through her contacts in the High Council. Amirah needed to know who had put a tail on her and why and if it had anything to do with what happened to Morgan. However, her concern grew when her contacts that usually always took her calls were suddenly unavailable upon hearing it was her.

Only two of the elder council members would take her call. They confirmed that her tail was from a government-backed supernatural monitoring agency. The agency was known as the Paranormal Supervision and Investigation agency or PSI for short. It was an amalgamation of the three other major worldwide agencies that had now united. This unification had come after the last incident that nearly caused a full-scale war amongst all the factions of earth, including the vampires and humans. None of her contacts could tell her who the agent was; all they knew was that he was one of the elite hunters they had taken out of retirement for this assignment.

The mention of the elite hunters was enough to make even the most powerful of vampire's shudder. They were terrifying hunting machines. Once on a supernatural creature's scent, they would not stop until their missions were completed successfully. They may hunt in elite teams, but one hunter was more than capable of taking down an entire hive of vampires.

Amirah shuddered, touching the thin scar near her collar bone, a reminder to never underestimate a hunter. Although there were rumors, no one really knew why these hunters were so powerful; some even thought they were half and halves.

Amirah had no other option; she had to call Grant, one of her sires. Surely two decades was long enough for him to get over his tantrum. Grant also happened to be the newly appointed second-in-charge of the Human Surveillance Alliance or HSA. The HSA was the supernatural equivalent of the PSI.

Grant's number rang for a long time; before his voice resonating with annoyance growled, hello into the receiver.

"Hello Grant," Amirah purred into the phone and was greeted by a frosty silence. "Do you have company?" She could hear there was another heartbeat beat in the room. But when he spoke again, it was gone. Grant must have moved away from whoever it was.

"What do you want, Amirah?" Grant asked. His tone letting her know two decades was not long enough for him to get over his anger.

"Still mad at me then?" she asked, hoping he would say the words she wanted to hear.

"No, Amirah, I got over all that a long time ago." His voice was flat, but she was not who he wanted to be talking to.

"Okay, then," she would let this go for now. "I need some information from the HSA."

"Of course, you do," he did not sound surprised that she wanted something from him yet again.

"I am being tailed by a PSI agent," she told him.

"So?" Grant asked her.

"So?" Hurt and anger shot through her like a hot rod. "Well, thanks a lot for your concern that I have an elite hunter trailing me."

"You should have led with the elite hunter part," Grant sounded a little more concerned. "Hold on."

She could hear him typing on a keyboard; he was quiet for a good few minutes.

"Amirah..." Grant's voice was now laced with concern. "It is not just any elite hunter; they have assigned to you," he was quiet for a bit. "It's Luka Brock."

Amirah swallowed and pressed her eyes shut. Every supernatural creature on this planet prepared themselves for this day. The day they knew there really was no such thing as the ultimate apex predator. Especially when nature proved a mere bird could take down the most venomous of snakes.

Amirah sat, staring at her phone for a while. She needed more information on Luka. But after a few more tries from various other contacts, all they could tell her was everything she already knew about the man. He was basically a legend in both supernatural and human circles. The man helped take down evil unbiasedly, whether they were supernatural or not. In fact, some of the vampire factions he had taken out she would actually like to give him a medal for.

Mmm... Maybe he could solve their new-age vampire problem and then their human counterparts. Focus Amirah. She could not remember when last she had felt this anxious. She had been tailed many times, kept under surveillance; hell, she even reigned supreme for nearly two decades forging her legacy of blood terror. During that time, she had come across her fair share of hunters. She retraced her scar. The only physical scar that had not healed on her body thanks to a hunter's blade forged with silver mined from the Okapi Grove and drenched with witch hazel. But she had never had a targeted killer set on her.

Pull it together, Amirah; you have survived plagues, wars, and terrors that would turn most people into dust with sheer fright. Dust… Amirah closed her eyes as images of Morgan disappearing before them swam in front of her. She looked to her mantle, and the pewter jar she had swept his ashes into. A thought struck her, what if…

She picked up the phone and called another branch of the HSA. It was two a.m. when her doorbell rang, and she admitted the Druid, or at least one of the Druids. No one knew if they were human, supernatural, half and halves, or really much about them. All anyone or thing knew about them was that they were like the Switzerland of the supernatural and human species. They never took sides, nor would they bow to any faction; they were also treated like Gods. They wore full-length black robes that allowed for only their pale blue eyes to peak out. Even their hands were covered by black silk gloves, and they never spoke, or at least, no one had ever heard one speak, or anyone not of the supreme level that is.

Without a word, the Druid opened a silver canister that appeared out of nowhere, or probably somewhere in his robe; Amirah craned her neck to see. He pulled out a vial that he popped open, taking out a long tube that he sucked up a few drops of liquid from the vile.

Amirah knew the drill; she knelt in front of him, tilted her head back, and allowed the Druid to drip a drop of the liquid onto her tongue. As it hit her tongue, it felt like Amirah had been punched in the gut. She coughed, grabbing her stomach and nearly losing her balance. After a while, the feeling settled, and she was able to stand up. Never had a sample affected her that way; what was it with blood lately?

The Druid's pale blue eyes stared at her, waiting for affirmation that she had what she needed to find her target. She nodded, and the Druid vanished. She did find it rude that they never used the door to leave. Amirah often felt like they were still floating around somewhere, watching. She shuddered at the thought before going off to change—she had a hunter to hunt, and the taste of his blood would lead her right to him. Vampires were a lot like canines, only where a canine needed the scent, vampires needed to taste the creature's blood.

Well, that was not hard at all, thought Amirah as she slipped open the lock on the apartment door. Wow, he really needed to up his security system as well as have words with the building committee as it was way too easy for the likes of her to get in here. But this apartment was fantastic; she loved the oak flooring and high ceilings. She had often wondered about this building. It was one of the oldest in the city; it was also always occupied. You had to know people of people and so on to ever get in, which meant the PSI was VERY well connected.

She stopped and plastered herself against the wall in the hallway, listening. She could hear the whirr of equipment, the hum of the air conditioning unit, and the refrigerator's engine. There was no other movement in the living area and kitchen, so she silently moved into the hallway that led to the study and bedrooms, stopping at the study door. It was wide open, so she popped her head around the door. It was tastefully furnished in period pieces. Her eyes scanned the large room with its traditional marble fireplace that she could picture curling in front of. She was about to step in when her ears picked up the sound of a heartbeat. Her eyes scanned the room. Luka was asleep on the large antique leather sofa; a fire was slowly starting to die in the fireplace. She stood at the open door, silently watching him, wondering how to approach him. He was a magnificent male specimen, Amirah thought as she admired his half-naked torso. He was ripped with powerful arms and legs, but not too overly muscled; Amirah felt something stir inside her. She gave herself a mental shake; it really had been a long time since she had had a man. Pity, this one may very turn out to be her enemy. She sighed softly before pulling herself back to reality and trying to decide the best way to approach him without it turning into a bloodbath. She needed his help and really did not want to have to rip his nice throat out.

Amirah was about to move into the room but froze as his deep voice warned her, "I would not step too far into this room if I were you."

That is when she heard it, a soft click, and she looked down—a pressure pad. She heard a very soft

23

whoosh. Her head turned to the side, and there it was a small but undoubtedly deadly weapon pointed at her head.

"The security in the building may not be up to code," Luka confirmed what she had thought in the most sarcastic tone, letting her know he knew the building security had weak points. "So, those of us residing here are forced to set up our own. Especially in Old Town." He cocked his head as he folded his arms across his chest and looked at her.

Amirah had to admit she was grudgingly impressed by him, and the fact that he had not flinched or reached for the weapon she knew was beneath the one cushion.

"Rumor has it I am your new charge." Their eyes met and held as they searched the other for some clue as to what they were dealing with here.

"The rumors are true," Luka drawled, keeping her pinned in his sight as she broke their eye contact to have a look around the well-stocked bookshelves of the old-world study.

FOUR

The Meet Cute

"IT'S A LOVELY APARTMENT," AMIRAH SAID CASUALLY. She tried to determine exactly what was pointed at her head and if she could move fast enough to avoid it piercing her skull.

"Thank you, I'm looking after it for a while. Now, are you going to tell me why you are breaking into and entering my home?" Luka watched her wearily; he could not believe she had snuck up on him like this. Images flashed through his mind, images he would instead not dredge up right now. But they were surfacing from a past experience when another vampire had managed to sneak up and catch him as well as his team off guard.

"I was curious as to who was tailing me, and why?" She looked back at him, questioningly with her most beguiling smile.

"You could have just called. Or at least, knocked on the front door instead of sneaking up on me," he watched her skillfully trying to figure out how to escape the trap she had stepped into. All he had to do was click the button on the remote he had in his hand crushed under his armpit. But to do that, he had to remove his hand from said armpit. Then she would notice just how much her creeping up on him had affected him. It was bad enough keeping his heartbeat steady, so the shock-waves had to go somewhere, and right now, that was his shaking hands.

"True," Amirah admitted. "I have never been very patient, especially when it comes to having to wait for a decent hour to visit humans."

"Ah, so this is just a visit, then?" he did not look convinced, and neither was he going to make this easy for her. He clearly did not trust her kind, just as she did not really trust his. As much as Amirah hated to do this, she was going to have to be the one to wave the white flag; okay, so she was technically in the wrong here.

"I want to know why you are tailing me." Amirah's eyes fell onto the folders lying on the coffee table in front of the couch.

"Because I was assigned to," he watched her frown at him; that was not the answer she was looking for, and he knew it.

"What other orders were you given that concerned me or any of my clan?" she asked him directly. Now that she knew he actually did have some really high-tech security, which was currently pointed at her, she felt she needed to be direct.

"I have no orders that pertain to your clan," he told her honestly and feeling steadier now, he disarmed the weapons with a click of the remote. Although it was very fleeting, her quick sigh of relief did not go unnoticed by him.

"So, you are just, what?" she wandered into the room cautiously and sat down on the other side of the couch. "Tailing me then?"

"Observing," Luka corrected her, "And making sure you are not dipping into your human client supply."

"What?" Amirah frowned at him; why would the PSI think she was doing that unless there had been some sort of write up with one of the agencies about her? "Have I been written up?"

"Not that I know of," Luka shrugged, grabbing up the folders on the coffee table to put them on the desk.

"Then none of this makes sense to me," Amirah made herself at home by curling her legs up onto the couch as if she were a long-time guest.

Luka swallowed as he watched her; she was gorgeous, and he found her to be one of the most attractive women he had ever seen.

"To be dead honest, it does not really make sense to me either," he was surprised at how easily that had slipped out. He knew he was not compelled, yet, for some reason; felt he could speak his mind to her. He could also see that his words had surprised her.

"I have not been assigned a high-profile case for a while now. I am on the medical disaster aversion team," he wandered back to the couch, picking up his T-shirt from the back of a chair and started to pull it on. "So, it was quite a surprise when the agency assigned me to you."

"You don't have to get dressed on my account," Amirah gave him an alluring smile, her eyes traveling the length of his frame, tracing the defined contours of his torso. He swallowed and clenched his jaw. He felt his body starting to respond to the touch of those breathtaking eyes traveling over his body. He cleared his throat and fought for control, distracting himself by pulling on his shirt. "Spoilsport," she cooed and then laughed as she noted his obvious discomfort before changing the subject.

"Did you have eyes on my apartment last night?" she asked him, switching from teasing seductress back to business faster than the speed of light.

"Yes," he answered, offering her a bottle of water.

"Did you see what happened to the man that came to my door?" Amirah already knew the answer to that question as she opened the water.

"Yes," Luka watched her, wondering where she was going with this, but intrigued as he really wanted to know what the hell had happened to her visitor. "Is this the part where you turn me into dust?"

The file on her did not list what her special vampire abilities were. In fact, he had wondered if that was why he was assigned to her to find out. But then again, she had been around for centuries, so why no one had found that out by now was a mystery in itself.

She looked at him confused at first, but that quickly turned to outrage as she spat, "You think I had something to do with that?" The look on his face said it all, but she turned it around by telling him, "I thought you might have had something to do with it!" She accused, her eyes darkening dangerously.

"Ah, so you did come here to kill me then?" she noted he did not flinch when he said that, and there was absolutely no fear either. He did not even stiffen into defense mode as most hunters would have done, asking that question.

"I came here for answers. But if the need did arise, I would take the necessary action," she informed him.

"Fair enough," Luka said, now even more impressed with her. God, she really was an incredible creature. Luka could not remember a time when he had ever been so intrigued by a woman.

"Have you ever seen anything like that before?" she asked him, her voice dropping, and for a moment, he could have sworn she had looked scared and a little vulnerable.

"No, I have not," Luka frowned and shook his head in contemplation. "I know of a few things that can kill a vampire outright, but nothing that can turn them to dust like that."

"Ash," Amirah corrected, drawing his attention back to her in surprise. "It was ash." Amirah looked towards her apartment, amazed that he had a clear view from his study into her dining room. "It was like he had been cremated right in front of me. Without any fire or heat around him."

"Did you pick up anything strange about him before he turned?" Luka was being drawn in; he was now definitely convinced there was more to him being assigned to Amirah than he was told.

"No," Amirah shook her head, staring into space as she remembered what happened, "But he was bleeding from his ears." She turned to look at him, her cheeks flushed. "The strange thing is that the blood smelt like it was rotting. But I could not detect anything in him to cause that kind of decay." She looked towards her apartment again, "And the blood that had dripped from him onto the floor turned to ash with him." She opened her hands and looked down at them as she remembered all of Morgan's blood staining them.

"Who was he?" Luka asked her, a weird feeling bubbled up in his chest, thinking about a tall man in her living room.

"Morgan," she told him, quite amazed that Luka did not already know that. "Surely, you should know that?"

"Why would I have needed to know about Morgan?" Luka asked a little too sharply, eliciting a weird look from Amirah. He looked away and went off to get her file, sure there was nothing in the information he had been given about Amirah that mentioned Morgan.

"I was his sire," she told Luka, drawing his full attention back to her. Amirah continued to search Luka's eyes, looking for clues that he was playing her as she had come to play him for information. Two things stood out about this man: he had secrets, which he would not give up quickly, and he did not lie; he was also a straight shooter.

"Okay, so he was part of your clan of vampires," Luka watched her; he had gone through all the files on her clan vampires, but there was nothing mentioned about Morgan. Maybe he was new and had not been documented yet. "When did you sire him?" Luka asked her.

"Around the year 1631, he was my sixth that I sired," she looked confusedly at Luka's look of surprise.

"That should be in your files," he yanked open the one desk drawer that was a neat array of folders. He flicked through them. "Did he go by any other name?" Luka asked her, starting to get a bad feeling.

"No, he was Morgan Grundling; his father was a

merchant trader in a small German village." She wandered over to the desk, craning her neck to see the files.

"I don't have one on him," Luka closed the drawer, not comfortable with her looking in his filing drawer.

"Maybe they did not send it over," Amirah suggested. Still, by what she was able to see in just that drawer, she very much doubted the agency would leave out any detail about her. She wondered how many other drawers were filled with information about her in this apartment. "Luka, what did they tell you about your current assignment?" Amirah asked him, playing with a very old fountain pen she found on his desk.

He watched her caress the antique pen, her long, elegantly groomed fingers gently playing with the quill. He swallowed as the heat started to gather in his gut. Get a grip, man! Luka admonished himself; he was like a hormonal teen lusting after his teacher. He snatched the pen from her hand and placed it back on its stand before answering, his voice a bit gruff. "Not much." He cleared his throat, ignoring her sultry smile that told him she knew full well the effect she was having on him. "It is a surveillance mission; nothing more as far as my orders have been," he plopped back against the office chair's plush leather chair, watching her perched at the end of the large oak desk.

"I see," Amirah stood up and leaned both hands onto the desk, looking down at him. "Why are they watching me now?" she asked perplexedly. "It is not as if I am a neophyte. I have been audited every year since the peace treaty after World War II," she pushed away from the desk and walked to the big bay window that looked directly into her flat. "I have complied with all the regulations and followed all the rules."

Anger started to spurt through her now. "So, why now?" she spun around as she did; she heard a click and froze, thinking Luka had reset the weapon. Her eyes flew to him accusingly, but he frowned back at her and raised his finger to his lips for her to be quiet. As soft as it was, he had heard it.

He indicated for her to use her super sense to find the source while his trained eyes scoured the room. He knew this apartment exceptionally well; there was not one inch he did not know, and he was sure it was not bugged. He did a scan every time he returned to the apartment after being out. He looked at Amirah suspiciously, but his gut told him whatever it was, was not introduced by her. The only other person to have been in his apartment was Jeff, but he had had eyes on him the entire time.

He moved just as silently and gracefully as she did. He was not sure if he was walking right into a trap, but once again, his gut told him if he was, it was not made by her. Or maybe that was just what he wanted to think because he knew the moment he laid eyes on her that he wanted her. She mesmerized him; perhaps that was her superpower—allure, like a siren. So trapped in his head, he nearly knocked her to the ground when she gently tapped him on the shoulder. She nimbly jumped back, avoiding his aggressive contact, hissing, "Easy there, big fella," her brow creased as she watched him go from wild-eyed to cool in under a second. "You are kind of jumpy; maybe I should take the lead," she whispered before indicating to the kitchen and trying to edge around him.

"I just had a vampire break into my house and sneak up on me. Now, there may be someone listening or worse, recording everything in my apartment," he whispered, holding her back. "So, hell yeah, I'm a bit jumpy," he ignored her raised eyebrows by deliberately stepping in front of her.

They silently edged into the kitchen; both standing dead still to listen. There was nothing there, or at least, nothing he could see. He looked over at Amirah; she had moved back into the darkened passage and was pointing to the counter. He looked down, but all he saw was the new spy-gear glasses. As Luka was about to pick them up, he could have sworn he saw something blue flicker on them, but before he could touch them, Amirah moved like lightning grabbing his hand. A shock zinged through his arm like he had touched a live wire. His eyes flew to Amirah's, who was looking just as shocked as he was; they stood there staring at each other dumbstruck, before quickly jumping apart.

Amirah's cheeks had a telling pink stain across them while the vein in Luka's neck throbbed. Needing the distraction, Amirah silently backed all the way down the hall, indicating for him to follow.

When he was in earshot, she asked, "So, why do you think we are both being watched?" Yes, something definitely was not right here. "I need your help, Luka," Amirah whispered as they stood trying to ignore the tension mounting between them. "I want to know what happened to Morgan, and I am sure you have your own demons to figure out," she pointed towards the glasses.

"I don't think that will work," Luka told her. "I am supposed to be monitoring you, not working with you."

"Well, it seems to me that we are both being played

here," she opened the front door, "There is something bigger going on here, Luka, and I think we need each other to figure it out."

The door clicked shut behind her. Luka stood staring at it while his mind raced with questions as his gut instinct was going into the banshee-screaming mode that Amirah was right.

FIVE

Joining Forces

AMIRAH DID NOT REALLY NEED TO REST; IT IS NOT THAT vampires did not need or could not rest. They just chose not to. Amirah had gone home after Luka's, changed, and went into the office, never being one to put things off until tomorrow. She needed to know what in the hell was going on. Vampires did not just dissolve into ash, paranormal agencies did not just put tails on supernatural creatures, and they most certainly did not spy on their own—okay, maybe they did that. But she could tell Luka had felt that something else was going on here too, something they were both being kept in the dark about.

One of the first things she needed to do was make sure the rest of her vampire clan were okay. Her vampire clan was her family; she mostly felt like a mother to the vampires she had sired. When one of them got hurt, it hurt her, too, in more ways than anyone knew.

Amirah stood watching the sunrise from her office. Her phone was pressed to her ear as she waited for Matthew to pick up, only to have it go through to voicemail. She closed her eyes, please, let him be okay. Jarod was the fourth of her clan not to answer their phone. As she was about to dial again, the phone rang. It was Jarod, and relief flooded through her. He was the most recent of her clan and the one she considered her baby. "Amirah?" his deep voice was like music to her ears. The relief that flooded her made tears sting her eyes. "What's up?" he asked her, his voice sounding a bit gruff, and that is when she realized he had been sleeping.

"Sorry. Did I wake you?" she asked him, smiling into the phone, knowing how much Jarod loved his sleep, unlike other vampires.

"It's no problem. I had to get up anyway. I have a marathon to prepare for." Even though he could probably outrun everyone at these runs, he never used his vampire abilities to do so. "So, are you going to tell me why you are so upset?"

She smiled, that was what you get for turning an empath; not much you could hide from them. "It's Morgan," her voice dropped. So much had happened since last night that she had not had much time to think about him. But it was hitting her now. It felt like she had just taken a bullet to the chest. "He is gone."

"Gone as in on a trip?" Jarod asked hopefully, but his voice held a catch that said he knew what she was about to say next.

"No, he died in my arms last night," Amirah's voice was soft and a bit scratchy, tears burning the back of her throat.

"What happened?" Jarod asked her.

"I want to get as many of the clan as I can on a conference call so I can tell you all at once," she ticked off his name when he said he would make sure he was available when she was ready. She made him promise to be careful, warning him that Morgan's death was not an accident.

Unlike other vampires, Amirah tried to keep track of her clan vampires. Sometimes though, she had to revert to social media stalking, but they knew she was trying. She even had a system for sending birthday reminders for each of them, which was a mission back in the day. Still, thanks to modern technology, she did not even have to do much. Minus Reginald and Morgan, she was left with thirty-three clan members, and she was determined to make sure none of them fall prey to whatever Morgan had.

By the time Rachel breezed into work, Amirah had already been there for four hours, scouring through her clan to make sure they were still alright. She had not been able to get hold of five of them. She had left messages on voicemail or through messaging apps for them and at their offices. She was truly on edge, not being able to contact some of her family members. Amirah smelled the coffee from the minute Rachel had stepped onto the office suit's private elevator. By the time Rachel's cheery face popped into her office, she could hardly wait to take the first sip of the special brew only Rachel knew how to make special.

"You are a lifesaver," Amirah hugged the warm mug to her before taking a swallow and letting the warm brew slide down her throat.

"Good morning to you too," Rachel leaned over the desk, frowning at Amirah's checklist.

"A bit early for your Christmas due diligence, isn't it?" Rachel asked as she started to clear up the mess

Amirah had made of her neatly arranged desk. Or at least, it was neatly arranged when Rachel had left the night before.

Amirah gave Rachel a shocked look; Amirah loved the holiday season. "My dear, dear girl, everyone knows it is never too early to prepare for the holiday season," she ran her pen down the list, shaking her head at the next vampire she had to call; she had deliberately left him for last—Johnny! He was such fun, to begin with, but then turned into a bit of a clinger. He still tried to worm his way back into her love life whenever he could. "No, this is not a Christmas listing; it is family politics," she told Rachel; she did not want to get her involved in whatever this was. Rachel had already had enough in her life; she did not need Amirah's drama.

"I thought I was family," Rachel looked hurt as she turned and made her way to the door.

"Of course, you are," Amirah said to her. After having found her six years ago, Rachel was like a daughter to her. Fighting for her life as a brute was trying to drag her into an alley.

"One of my clan vampires, Morgan, died last night," Amirah told her, "so, I have to let the rest know. I was going to come and tell you when I was done talking to Johnny." Amirah knew that Rachel would understand her exasperation when she mentioned Johnny's name. Rachel shuddered as she had not met all of Amirah's many clan vampires, but she had Johnny, and she did not like him.

She ran over and gave Amirah a hug. "I'm so sorry, Amirah," Rachel then left Amirah to her phone call.

Unlike most of her other clan members, Johnny never let the phone ring too long before answering it.

"Amirah," Johnny drawled from the other end of the phone. "How nice to hear from you."

"Hello, Johnny," Amirah was not fooled by his calm persona.

"To what do I owe the pleasure of your call?" he asked her a bit frostily.

Here we go again! Amirah sighed.

"I was just calling to find out if you were okay and how you were doing?" she asked, not sure if she really wanted to tell him about Morgan.

"I am great," he said enthusiastically. "In fact, I guess you could say life is perfect for me at the moment." He waited for a reaction. "I have a new woman in my life, and she is mind-blowing…" his voice dropped conspiratorially as he continued, "If you know what I mean?"

Amirah shook her head. She really wished Johnny would use messaging, but he refused. It really would make keeping in contact with him much easier for her.

"Well, I am so glad to hear that, Johnny," she sorted through the files on her desk, finally finding the one to do with the mixer.

"You deserve every happiness. Just remember to follow the rules and stay safe," she said to him, her mind preoccupied with the file in front of her.

"I heard about Morgan," Johnny said, his voice taking on a more serious lilt and grabbing her full attention again.

"How did you hear about Morgan?" Something in his voice made the hair on her arms stand on end, and her instincts tingle. No, she was just being overly suspicious. She knew Johnny was clingy, jealous, and could be a bit sneaky, but he had always liked Morgan. She also did not think Johnny could hurt anyone, but her neck hair was even standing on end.

"Grant," Johnny told her, yet there was still something in his voice that she did not like. He was also a lot cockier and surer of himself than usual.

"We do work together now, you know," he added what she thought was merely for good measure; she had a sneaky feeling he was not telling her everything.

"Yes, I was told," Amirah said. "Congratulations on getting that position, by the way."

"Thank you. I did get your gift basket. Very thoughtful of you," Johnny told her. "Grant also told me that there was still no one new in your life."

Johnny tried to steer the conversation back to relationships, as he always did.

"You know, I am always here if you need ..." he lowered his voice to what she used to think of as his sexy lilt but now only left her cold, "a bit of Johnny love."

She wanted to laugh but refrained. He did annoy her. Johnny was clingy and needy and tried to make her jealous every chance he got, but he was still one of hers. She knew too that she had really hurt him when she moved their relationship into a platonic one.

"Listen, Johnny, Morgan did not die in an accident or of natural causes. As yet, I don't know what killed him. So, I need you to be extra careful, okay?"

"So, you do still care?" he moved the conversation back to him again. "Maybe even more than you still realize?"

"Johnny, not this again. I have had a terrible night, and I am really not ..." the door to her office swung open. Her heart skipped a beat as her pulse quickened when the tall, rugged hunter stepped into her line of sight.

She nearly did not notice that he had actually pushed Rachel into her office, plastered against the door, and shouting at him, "Sir, you really cannot go in there."

But there he was; their eyes met and held from across the room. Without another word or thought, Amirah put the phone down, cutting off Johnny, who was once again pouring his heart out to Amirah.

"I am so sorry, Amirah," Rachel extracted herself from the door and stepped around the rude man, trying to cut him off once again. "But this Neanderthal just barged his way through here." Rachel's cheeks were flushed in outrage that this stranger had had the gall to ignore her. "Now, I understand why you try to empower women," she placed her hands on her hips, standing her ground, and glared at the man gawking at her boss.

Amirah and Luka stared at each other; something stirred inside her, but before she could figure out what, she was distracted by the shrill ring of her mobile phone. The moment was gone, and the connection was broken as she looked at her phone—Johnny's name flashed on the screen. She hit ignore and took a quick second to compose herself. What was it about this hunter that stirred her up inside?

Not waiting for an invite, Luka leaned over, grabbed Rachel by her waist, lifting her up. Midway, he stopped and curiously looked at her. His grip loosened and gentled as he put her down as softly as he could but to one side so he could make his way further into the office. Without a word, Amirah watched him make himself comfortable in one of the chairs in front of her desk.

"I don't believe we had an appointment," Amirah said, watching a slow smile spread across his face. He was a very manly male, Amirah thought, as her pulse started to race again.

"I know, right?" he meaningfully raised his eyebrows. "Uninvited guests can be quite annoying, especially when they just let themselves in unannounced."

"Touché," Amirah smiled back at him, her attention caught by her upset assistant barreling towards them.

"So, you know this caveman?" Rachel scathed. "I hope he is here for a lesson in manners and how to make an appointment. Or maybe how to read as it clearly states on the office door, by appointment only." Rachel's leaned in on Luka for which she received one of his most alluring smiles. "Your charming He-man smiles, don't fool me, buster."

"It's okay, Rachel," Amirah stood up, amused, a bit embarrassed, and proud at how her assistant had tackled a man who topped the girl by a good foot, not to mention weight class. "I can take it from here."

Rachel stood glaring at the man. She looked up at Amirah, saying as she flounced out the room, "Your first appointment will be here soon," Rachel gently closed the door behind her.

"Wow!" Luka whistled. "Now I see why you would keep her around."

He was clearly impressed by the girl, as not many people stood up to him. "Feisty for a human, isn't she?" he shook his head, watching Amirah once again hit ignore on her mobile phone. "Now, I see what they mean by a mama bear."

Amirah frowned at him. "Actually, I am more like a mom to her," Amirah told him before sitting back in her chair. "So, Luka, what brings you to my office today?"

He pointed to his earpiece in a warning. Amirah gave a nod of understanding as he said, "It seems that your two unscheduled visits last night raised a few red flags and drew a lot of attention from the powers that be."

"Two visits…?" she asked cautiously.

"Yes, it seems my bosses want to know about your clan member turning to dust," she was about to correct him, but he put his finger to his lips, stopping her. "They also want to know why you missed our earlier agreed upon meeting last night and decided to drop by at the early hours of this morning instead," his eyes narrowed in on her warningly.

Amirah watched him; she was impressed and even more intrigued by him now. She also had an inkling that he was going to help her as he clearly did not trust his powers that be. So, she would play along and see where it would lead as both of them needed answers. "After what happened, it took me a while to get it together," she decided to play the grieving mother vampire card before continuing. "I guess I lost track of time and did not realize how late it actually was," she gave him a tantalizing smile.

"What about your unfortunate visitor?" Luka asked her after being prompted by what she made out as a female voice in his ear. Figures, Amirah thought before catching herself, why the hell would I even care?

"What do you want to know?" she honed in on his conversation. Yes, it was rude, but so was talking about her as if she was not there.

"Last night, you mentioned your visitor was a

vampire. All sires of historical vampires need to be registered, yet we have no record of anyone you sired by the name Morgan."

Amirah still found that a bit weird as she knew Morgan was registered or could not work as a scientist. In fact, he had been helping to try and combat some of the more vicious viruses on the planet. She had yet to mention that to Luka. She was still not too sure about his motives, and although it may seem she had given him a lot of information, she had not.

"I find that hard to believe," Amirah said, not at all fazed by the accusation that she had turned a human without consequence. "Morgan has been around for over three centuries."

"Yet, there is no record of him at either the PSI or the HAS," Luka's expression changed as soon as he was fed that information. Amirah still could not get a read on him, so she was unsure whether he was looking at her suspiciously or not, but he was most definitely contemplating something. His entire demeanor had changed, only Amirah did not know what he was thinking.

"Well, then I think you should all look again because he has been around forever." This was getting ridiculous; now, obviously, if his records were no longer there, they had been removed for some reason. She needed to wrap this up and quickly so she could get over to Morgan's apartment. In fact, she should have gone straight there last night instead of hunting down Luka. "Now, if there is nothing further, I suggest you tell your little birdie in your ear to do her job and find those records." Amirah started fidgeting with the files on her desk. She needed him out of her office if he was not going to help her so she could get to Morgan's apartment. "If you don't mind showing yourself out, I have work to do." She dismissed him. Well, tried to anyway as he stood up slowly and leaned over her desk.

"No, I don't think so," Luka said quietly. "We have work to do, and if I am going to help you, you are going to clear your schedule for the day. Then we are going to continue working our way through your list of clan members." He smiled at the shocked look on her face. "I can read upside down."

"Do I have a choice?" she asked him, picking up her list of clan members from her desk as he escorted her out of her office.

"Not really as it seems I am to offer you my coopera-tion in looking into the death of this mysterious Morgan." As he ushered her out of the door, saying, "Oh and I am going to need a copy of that list of all your clan members. Including the years in which they were turned."

As they walked out of the office, Amirah informed Rachel to reschedule all her appointments due to a family emergency. Before they could leave the office, a call came through to Rachel, and she called out to Luka, "Tarzan, it is for you." Luka's eyebrows shot up; Rachel clearly did not like him.

"Rachel, don't be disrespectful," Amirah admon-ished her assistant.

"Fine," Rachel looked at Luka before saying sarcasti-cally, "Mr. Tarzan, there is a call for you."

"I like her," Sophie whispered in his ear before Luka switched her off, his eyes locked with Amirah, whose lips twitched, confirming his suspicion that she could hear Sophie in his ear. "Hello." Luka barked into the receiver.

SIX

Road Trip

"Luka, General Trent here," Luka instantly stiffened into position. Just as any dutiful soldier would do when addressed by a superior officer.

"Good morning, sir," Luka addressed the general.

"As you know by now, your paranormal charge has come up on our radar as a person of interest," the general kept his voice low. "We want you to give her all the support she needs to figure out what happened to the victim from last night." Luka frowned at the man's use of the word victim; his senses started to tingle again. He realized where this conversation was about to go. "All information gathered comes straight to my office, is that clear, soldier?" the general ordered.

"Yes, sir," Luka answered dutifully.

"Oh, and Luka…" the general's voice dropped even lower, "should the PNC, at any point, become hostile or you feel is a threat in any way, you are to deal with it with whatever force you deem necessary. Are your orders clear, soldier?"

"Yes, sir, loud and clear, sir," Luka confirmed he had

understood before the line on the other side went dead. His eyes met Amirah's from across the room, where she stood watching him while holding open the elevator. Had she heard? He tapped his earpiece to switch it back on, but there was nothing. Odd, he thought. He stepped into the elevator and pulled out his mobile phone. There was no signal on it either.

Luka tapped his earpiece upon exiting the building. It was still dead. He looked at his mobile phone, still no signal. He frowned, turning to Amirah, and asked, "Do you have any cell service?"

Amirah pulled her phone from her coat pocket, "Yes, I do."

"That's odd," Luka led Amirah to his sleek pickup truck parked in the front of her building and opened the door for her.

"Did you forget to pay your bill?" Amirah asked him with a grin.

"Well, considering I do not pay for this phone, it is not up to me to pay it, but I don't even have any bars," he hopped into the driver's seat and tapped at his earpiece again.

"Mites?" Amirah asked with a raised eyebrow

"What?" Luka was preoccupied with pulling out of the parking space and figuring out what had happened to his communication devices.

"You keep fiddling with your ear," Amirah gestured with her finger and tapped her ear. "So, I thought maybe you had mites or something," she laughed at the look on his face.

"Mites?" he asked her mortified. "That is something I don't think I have ever had. Although I have been to some shady places where I had to swim through the most awful water." Luka laughed as he watched her visibly shudder at that image.

"Rather, you than me," Amirah could think of nothing worse than wading through some putrid bodies of water. "But seriously, is everything okay?" She looked at him with something that seemed to Luka like genuine concern.

"I'm fine. I was…" before Luka could finish, a high-pitched sound screamed through his eardrum, making even Amirah cover her ears and moan "Holy…" Luka swerved to the side of the road and slammed on breaks as he yanked his earpiece out of his ear.

"What the hell was that?" Amirah asked, glaring down at the tiny earpiece on his lap. Her ears felt like someone had sliced through them with a razor blade. She could only imagine how his eardrums must be feeling.

Luka picked the earpiece up and turned it over, looking at it perplexed. "I am not sure," he opened the car window and threw the gadget out. "But until I figure out what the hell is going on, let's not have this thing anywhere near us." With that, he pulled the pickup back onto the road, heading toward their first stop.

"Do me a favor and let me know when my phone gets a signal again as we are about to leave the city limits." Amirah nodded and picked up his phone, noting the route on his car's GPS.

"I see you have been doing your homework," Amirah pointed to the address on the screen; it was the address of one of her clan. As she noticed the GPS was not working, she frowned and looked at him. "I think you are having technical difficulties," Amirah tapped the touch screen with a long red nail, but the display did not change.

"Exactly what I have been thinking since we got off your elevator," he gave her a suspicious look.

"Wait a minute…" Amirah did not like what he was insinuating, "You seriously do not think I had anything to do with all your spy gear going awry?"

"What am I supposed to think?" he asked her cautiously. "Your phone is fine. Yet, all my communications devices mysteriously malfunction as we leave to find one of YOUR clan vampires." He glanced at her now tense shoulders. He could practically feel her starting to prickle.

"First, I am in YOUR vehicle. Unarmed and have told no one where I am going because I did NOT KNOW where we were going," she fiddled in her handbag, pulling out her phone. "Second, I am not the one with all the high-tech gadgets or know-how to pull off being able to somehow disable your toys. I am not the one with some tech genius in my ear and…" she stopped mid-rant.

He glanced at her shaking her phone and then trying different positions in the air with it. "I don't have any signal," her eyes flew around to him, filled with accusations of her own now. "If this is some kind of joke…" she warned him. "I don't have a signal either, and I have traveled this route many times with a perfect signal." Amirah tried to dial a few numbers on her phone, but nothing went through. Unease shrouded her like a heavy coat around her shoulders.

"What do you mean you don't have any signal? Outside your building, you had a signal." Luka once again pulled over onto the side of the road, taking her phone. "Dammit."

"Maybe there is a problem with the towers," Amirah said hopefully. "We are jumpy because of those stupid spy goggles of yours." The mention of the glasses had her searching the car with her eyes.

"I did not bring them with me as I was not comfortable with them," he held his finger to his lips as he carefully started sifting through the car for any listening or spying devices. "I feel like Clark Kent when I wear them."

Amirah looked at him, confused, "Who," she asked him, "is Clark Kent?"

"You know, Superman." He stopped his searching to look at her to see if she was joking.

She shrugged and shook her head.

"You're joking, right?" he asked her, as everyone had evidently heard of Superman. Well, Sophie was going to be disappointed that her hero, Amirah, did not know who Superman was.

"What are you doing?" Amirah asked him as he patted down his car like it had just beeped through a metal detector at an airport.

"Playing the drums. What does it look like I am doing?" he said sarcastically, making her drawback and raise her eyebrows indignantly.

A slow smile lifted the one side of his mouth as he leaned in towards her. Her eyes widened as his lips drew closer to her ear. He could see the vein in her neck pulse. The urge to press his lips against it was so great he nearly gave in to it; his body immediately reacted to the thought. He swallowed hard as her scent tantalized his nostrils, wrapping around him. He almost lost himself in her only to be yanked back to reality by the sound of a car zooming by them. The car was going so fast the pickup shook in its wake. He sat back down in his seat, taking a few seconds to compose himself—that was not good. All he had wanted to do was whisper in her ear, he was looking for a tracking device, but the minute he had gotten close to her, he almost lost control of his senses. This was strictly work. Get a hold of yourself, Luka. Stop acting like a horny teenager every time she so much as looks at you!

Not wanting to get too close before he had completely regained control over his traitorous libido, he found a pen and an old receipt upon which he wrote:

Checking for listening devices or other spy gear toys.

She nodded and cleared her throat. Her cheeks had a rosy flush to them, and her vein still pulsed a little erratically in her neck. Luka smiled to himself, knowing that nothing would ever come of it. Not only was this business, but there was also the matter of her being a vampire. But it felt good knowing he was not the only one affected by their proximity.

Amirah shook her head before snatching the pen from him to write beneath his scrawl:

Drive. I will look. That way, the engine noise will drown out the shuffling as you sound like a chicken scratching up roots.

He laughed as did she, breaking up the tension in the car.

"Why are we going to Josh's and not Morgan's?" Amirah asked Luka. She had given Luka Morgan's address early that morning.

"I went there, and no Morgan was living there or had ever lived there," he told her. "Only whoever tried to erase Morgan did not do an excellent job of clearing out all the trash." He reached into his pocket and drew out a photo of Morgan he gave Amirah. "I found this in the dumpster behind the building."

As Luka drove towards the countryside, Amirah sat back and concentrated. She closed her eyes, blocking out all the surrounding noise. After what Luka had just told her about Morgan's life being erased, it was glaringly apparent she was now a target for whatever was going on here. She fought to clear and quiet her mind, and then she focused her attention on sounds that were out of place. At first, she could detect nothing out of the ordinary. She went deeper and let her sense travel around the car. There was something, the faintest of a beep. She focused a little more, trying to figure out the direction. She allowed her mind to float towards the sound, like trying to fix the sound's position. Her hand shot up and hit the dashboard; her eyes flew open. Luka was staring at her like she had two heads.

"What the hell?" he breathed. "You nearly gave me a heart attack." His eyes followed her arm where her hand was pinned to the glove compartment. His brow creased as their eyes locked. She gave the nod. He understood. She moved her hand from the latch. They both stared at the inside. They could see nothing out of place. She looked around and noticed they had stopped outside a familiar house. It belonged to Josh, one of her clan, and the first one on her list who had not answered his phone or his messages. According to his Facebook, he had updated it two days ago and his Twitter right after that.

As they stepped out of the car, a smell caught her attention. One that set off alarm bells and was all too familiar, yet it was one she still could not identify. It put all her senses on high alert. It also brought back a flood of memories that she fought off while fighting off the urge to charge headlong into Josh's house. That smell never had a good ending and had ripped her family apart more than once in her long lifetime.

Her instincts on high alert, she barked at Luka, "Something is not right, stay in the car," she ordered, her mind so set on getting into Josh's house that she did not see the look on Luka's face.

"I don't think so, sweetheart," Luka's angry voice tickled her ear, making her jump. She looked around. She had been so intent on following that scent and hoping it would not lead her to Josh's front door, she did not hear Luka behind her.

"What?" she hissed back, annoyed that he had stayed in the car like she had told him to.

"My mission, my rules. And NO ONE, especially not the likes of you, tells me to stay in the car." Ignoring her, he stepped around her and walked up to the front door, stopping to reach for his weapon as soon as he noticed it was slightly open.

Anger spurted through Amirah at his arrogance, and undeniable need to be a prime alpha. She stormed up the steps ready to lay into him, only to freeze as she noted the open door and how strong that weird scent had become. Amirah and Luka looked at each other, and then back at the door, silent and listening for movement inside. A mutual nod put them back into sync as they entered the house.

Amirah's heart pounded as they found the living room ripped apart. Her eyes scanned the room, a deep fear starting to claw at her gut. She had seen this scene before, actually; she had lived it—twice. Tears stung her eyes while they took in the room, seeing all his beautiful antique pieces ripped apart. Her chin tilted slightly as her vampire senses, skillfully collected information about the room. This must-have happened within the last day because his Facebook page was last updated two days.

"Amirah," Luka shouted from another room in the house. There was something in his voice that had her using her super-speed to find him. He was kneeling in Josh's kitchen, looking down at a pile of ash.

SEVEN

The Evil in the Air

"Is this what I think it is?" Luka asked her, knowing the answer by the stricken look on her face.

She knelt down beside him, picking up a bit of the ash between her fingers. Luka watched her struggle with her emotions, her head tilting up slightly as she took in the surrounding scents. "Yes," she whispered. "I think so. His scent is all over the kitchen."

"I'm so sorry, Amirah," he reached out to her. She looked up at him and nodded. "You know that I will have to call this in?" Luka did not want to call this in. In fact, every instinct in his body screamed at him not to, but until he had proof that his agency was involved, he needed to follow protocol.

Again, Amirah nodded, "I need to do the same."

Luka stood and helped Amirah to her feet before reaching for his phone; his brows creasing, he turned to her, "Was that a phone I spotted in the living room?" He asked as she nodded. He understood that she did not want to speak right now. The instant she had seen the pile of ash on the floor, he saw the emotion flicker in her eyes. There was sorrow, but also something else that had baffled him since she tried to order him back into the car—dread. He knew what dread looked like and felt it to the very core of his being. The minute he had stepped out of the pickup, he had felt something evil in the air. The same evil that had hung in the air on that fateful day Luka knew would forever be etched in his mind.

"I don't understand?" Amirah growled and shook her mobile phone. "I have always had reception here." This could not be good. But maybe Amirah was right, and there was a problem with the cell towers. He followed Amirah into the living room, where she asked him to look up a number on her useless mobile phone for someone called Grant. He did so, wondering why she had not password protected her phone.

~ ~ ~

"So, Josh built this place?" Luka was impressed. The house was laid out nicely, old school but with a modern twist. "Your clan is quite an impressive bunch. Lawyers, doctors, scientists, university professors, and architects." Luka and Amirah waited patiently for the HSA and PSI forensic teams to offer them protective gloves, suits, and booties to wear.

"Yes, I am rather proud of what they have achieved," Amirah snapped on the latex gloves before preceding Luka back into Josh's house.

They had done a complete but skillful snoop of the house before their teams had arrived on the scene, and then dutifully waited outside for them.

"Do you think we could snag a bit of the ash?"

Amirah asked him, her voice low, but before Luka could answer, a perky young voice piped in from behind them.

"I'm afraid not that would be against protocols…" Amirah and Luka turned around, both startled at how this slip of a girl had snuck up on them. "For both the HSA and PSI." She scrunched up her clean make-up free young face. Her hair scraped back into a long plait, while dark-rimmed glasses magnified the girl's big brown eyes and thick, sooty lashes. "I'm Sophie," the girl stuck out her hand to give Amirah's a vigorous shake. "The one usually in Luka's ear when he is not chucking me out onto the motorway." She punched Luka in the arm. "Thanks for that, by the way; you gave me quite the headache."

"Will you excuse us for a second, please, Amirah?" Luka did not wait for her reply before dragging Sophie down to the end of the garden. "What are you doing here, Soph?" Luka stared down at her, not happy with her being here when she was not sufficiently trained to handle PNCs. "The house is full of…" before she could finish, she blurted out.

"Paranormal Creatures or PNCs." She pushed her glasses up the bridge of her nose. "I am trained enough, and besides, this is their forensic team; they are harmless." She looked towards the door. "Well, at least I assume they are." She looked back at Luka, making her cute little "yay" face. Before he could go into full-blown lecture mode, Amirah called him from the door. He indicated he was on his way.

"I am not happy about this, and we will discuss this further," he started back up the path to the front door. "Stay close to our team or me," he stopped her with a last command. "Do not at any time find yourself alone with a PNC. Is that clear?"

She looked up at him and saluted, "Yes, sir, crystal clear, sir." She glared back at him before scooping up her kit and walking inside. She stopped next to Amirah, who was watching them from the front door. "It is great to meet you," she smiled at Amirah. "I am so sorry about Josh." Then she disappeared into the house.

"You were a little harsh on her," Amirah spat at him.

"I don't think she concerns you," Luka's tone told Amirah that he would not pursue this line of conversation with her. "Did you find anything?" he changed the subject, ignoring her narrowed eyes and the fact that if she was a cat, her hair would be fully raised on her back.

"I did actually," Amirah was seething. She had heard every word Luka had said to Sophie. She knew she was being rude listening in, but the girl seemed to think Luka's earpiece was working when they were in the pickup truck. Yet, he had said he could not hear anything. Did he orchestrate that high-pitched noise the device made and get rid of it deliberately? She shook her head. She was being ridiculous. Why would he have done that? There was no reason for it. Still, it was wise to keep her guard up.

She was learning that it was easy for her to let it down with Luka. She had learned the hard way that you could not trust humans. She really did not like his macho brutish attitude either; she had known the moment she laid eyes on him that he always had to be the alpha, his way or the highway.

~ ~ ~

"What the hell are they doing?" Luka stopped as they passed the guest bedroom. Vampires were standing in the middle of the room, just licking their lips.

"It's called scenting," Sophie popped up, seemingly out of nowhere again.

"Wow, you really are a little jack in the box, popping up when you least expect it," Amirah laughed at the youthful woman who grinned back at her. "She is right," Amirah told Luka.

"By scenting the air, they can recreate who was in the room and their movements around the room," Sophie explained the process to Luka.

"I'm impressed," Amirah applauded Sophie. "You really know your stuff. Doesn't she, Luka?" Amirah drawled, lifting her eyebrow with a told-you-so look. "You remind me so much of Rachel, my assistant," Amirah told her, observing the young woman. "It's uncanny; you two could be related."

"Is that something you can all do?" he asked, ignoring Amirah's insinuation and missing the hurt look in Sophie's eyes. He also wanted to remove Amirah's focus off Sophie.

"Yes," was all Amirah said, giving Sophie an encouraging shoulder squeeze that did not go unnoticed by Luka, nor did Amirah's glare, followed by a headshake.

"What?" Luka asked her, unaware of what he had just done.

"You are such a clueless ape," Amirah hissed before marching off towards the main bedroom.

Wow, what had crawled up her wrong end? Here he thought vampire women may be more evolved than human women. Seems they were the same, no matter the species. He sighed and followed Amirah into the main bedroom, stopping as he stepped over the threshold. His skin prickled, his gut clenched, an image he could not quite hold on to skittered across his mind, a Deja Vu clip complete with a familiar acrid smell.

He looked up to find Amirah watching him. She did not say a word, but he could see she was feeling it too. The room had more closets in it that one person could ever need in a bedroom. There were some photographs on the wall and a framed picture of Amirah on the nightstand. Luka's eyes fell on the picture. Even in her photos, she was alluring and drew a man in. Luka had admired the picture earlier on in the day when they had first let themselves into Josh's house. But something seemed different about the picture. He picked it up, frowning at it. He turned it over. The frame was the same, as was the picture, but something was definitely out of place.

"Josh loved photography and was always snapping pictures, especially when you least expected it." She took the picture from Luka and smiled at it. "This was the day Josh finally came out to me." As Amirah put the photo back down, she gave a soft laugh saying. "I see he changed the picture frame."

Luka's eyes shot to picture, and that is when he noticed the four tiny black dots placed neatly around the picture. The frame had been changed, but not by Josh; it had been changed within the last couple of hours. This meant that someone here thought there was still unfinished business and were confident that business would return to this house. It also meant if there was one bug, there were a lot more, as well as cameras. Which were also not there when Amirah and Luka entered the house earlier.

"I think we are being called," Luka grabbed Amirah's arm to steer her out of the bedroom.

"What the…" she hissed. She had had enough of his caveman attitude. She dug her heels in and spun herself out of his grasp to face him angrily. Her anger simmering down when she saw him raise his finger to his lips and tap his ear.

"How about a bottle of water to go with that temper?" Luka suggested in a low voice before continuing to steer her out of the house and down to his pickup. He pulled two drinks of water from the cooler box in the truck's bed.

"What the hell was that?" Amirah asked, still a little angry at his Neanderthal tactics.

"Tell me about the picture frame," Luka opened the cap on the water bottle. He stood with his back against the truck, making sure Amirah stood in front of him so he could scan the house. At first, he had thought nothing of it, but he and Amirah were definitely being watched by the two agents that seemed to be everywhere they were.

"What does Josh's picture frame have to do with anything?" Amirah hissed, taking a swig of the water; if she did not need his help, she would gladly knock that male arrogance and dominant he-man attitude out of him.

"You were right. The frame was changed, but within the last couple of hours." he whispered, not sure if they could be heard from where they were.

Her eyes widened as what he was saying sunk in. How the hell had she wandered into some Jason Bourne type scenario. "It looked similar to the original one, except for the decorations and missing crack on the back of it." Her voice had dropped to that tone he noticed her using whenever she whispered to him when others were around.

"Does that work?" he asked her while watching the two agents at the front of the house looking through the garden.

"What work?" she asked him.

"That low tone you speak in whenever you don't want someone around us to hear you," he smiled, amused at the shocked expression on her face.

"So, you are not just all brawn after all," she looked impressed, "Sometimes." She said honestly, not ready to let him in on all her secrets or abilities.

"Great," he took the last swallow on his water. "You will need to stop using it inside and whisper to me normally that you have a lead." He placed his empty bottle back into his truck. "You also need to want to go because being inside the house is getting too much for you."

"Seriously?" her annoyance was back. Yes, she was really upset about Josh, and she would grieve for him— hard—in her own time. But right now, she was riding on her anger because it was that anger that was stopping her from falling to pieces in grief and fear for the rest of her clan. From the minute Morgan had turned to ash in her arms, she had had the feeling that whatever this was, it was aimed at her.

"Because I am a woman, I have to get all gooey and emotional?" she lashed out at Luka. "Women too, can be strong and driven. It is women who ultimately give birth to you brutes that think you can push us around."

She seethed, her eyes wild with anger, grief, and even fear, Luka noted as he watched her. She was magnificent, he thought, once again caught in her alluring spell. She was fierce, brave, and protective—she was a queen! Luka gave himself a mental shake—get a grip, man. He could stand here all day and watch her vent in pure anger, but right now, they were being watched and probably listened to. Until they knew what was going on or who they could trust, they had to stick together.

"Calm down, Poppy Stanton!" Luka took her water bottle from her. "We need to leave, now."

EIGHT

Back From the Dead

HER CHEEKS FLUSHED WITH HER RECENT OUTBURST, Amirah glared at him, wanting to stay mad at him but he made sense. He was also right; she found it difficult to be in the house right now, and his ploy to get them out had hit a little too close to a nerve.

"I don't think this is only a forensics team," he told her as they walked back towards the house. "There are more than a few surveillance experts among them parading as part of the forensic team."

Amirah's eyes followed where Luka steered her, trying to keep from looking suspicious the way Luka did. He had been in this spy versus spy game a lot longer than her. But she knew a thing or two about being stealthy and sneaky.

"So, you know who Poppy Stanton is?" Amirah teased him. "What... did you do women's studies in college?" She laughed at the look he gave her.

"No, but we had to study everyone who made an impact or had a significant change in the world or politics or was involved in radical movements," he told her before quickly adding for good measure. "But, I admired what she and Lucretia Mott started. They stood up for what they believed in and were not afraid to be heard."

Something inside Amirah shifted and warmed as she looked up at Luka when he stood aside for her to enter the room first. He had said that with genuine admiration and no sarcasm or chauvinistic undertones, so unlike what she would expect from a man like him. She was thinking there really was a lot more to Luka than met the eye.

"Okay, you're up," Luka whispered to her as they entered the kitchen. She noted some key forensic teams gathered together. They also seemed a little jumpy when she and Luka walked in, or that could just have been her suspicious nature making it seem as if they were.

"We are going to head off," Luka started the conversation with the team, getting the attention of the person he wanted to. Sophie.

"Where are you headed next?" Sophie all but bounced towards them like an enthusiastic little puppy, and, for the first time since he had met her, Luka did not trust her. Amirah could feel Luka tense up, so she moved quickly, digging her long nails into her palm. The searing pain made her eyes water.

"We are done here, and I really cannot take being in this house with all its memories for much longer," Amirah let a tear spill onto her cheek for effect. "I also think I have another lead. There was more than one person in this house at the time Josh died."

"Well, let me come with you guys," Sophie said excitedly. "I would love to get the field practice, and I could be of some help."

"I'm sorry, Soph," Luka stepped between Sophie

and Amirah. He may suspect Sophie, but that did not mean he wanted her to become Amirah's next meal either. "But, I think you are best off with the forensic team for now."

Sophie looked hurt but backed down, reached into her pocket, and handed Luka a new earpiece set. "This is for you, and there is one specially designed for Amirah," Sophie pointed to the different earpieces. "The agency wants both of you to be visible to them at all times. They do not know what we are dealing with here."

Before they left, Sophie grabbed Luka in a big hug and whispered to him, "Be careful." Then did the same to Amirah, stating, "Sorry, I'm a hugger, and I just want both of you to be safe."

～～～

"She is quite the bundle of energy and emotions," Amirah stated as they got into the pickup.

"Yup," Luka agreed and turned on the engine. "She is also a cunning little genius." He pulled a small mobile phone from his pocket before looking at Amirah, "What did you get for Christmas?"

Amirah looked at him for a second before patting her coat pocket and finding a similar phone in hers. "How the heck did she do that?" Amirah turned the small phone around, looking at it. "Is she a witch because I didn't even feel her do that."

"She's a thief," Luka told a very surprised Amirah. "I caught her trying to pickpocket me."

"Ah, no one can outsmart the great Luka Brock," Amirah mocked.

"Actually, she did," he got another shocked look from Amirah. "I was about to make a call when I noticed my phone was gone. The only reason I found it again was because the agency could track it for me." He laughed as he remembered the first day he had met Sophie. "She was as slippery as an eel and as vicious as a bear."

"Turn onto junction twelve," Amirah told him. "I think I know where to find who was in the house with Josh."

"We are being followed," Luka told her, grabbing her arm as she went to look behind them. "I know you want to, but don't look back." He reached past her and pulled down her visor. "Use the mirrors." He indicated to the side mirror, "White sedan four cars back."

"White?" Amirah raised her eyebrows. "Aren't they usually black sedans, SUVs, or some flashy sports car?"

"Maybe for the FBI, CIA, or James Bond," he corrected her. "Both the HSA and PSI use white cars as they are statistically the most common color car on the road."

"Smart," Amirah said, trying to find the white sedan. "Okay, I see it. They could have given the agents a better car. What is that a Prius?"

"Well, what better way to blend in than with a Prius?" Luka and Amirah looked at each smiling at the thought of agents stuck in a Prius rather than a flashy James Bond car or Men-in-Black type SUV.

"How do you know it is not just a soccer mom?" Amirah asked, trying to zoom in on the driver. Still, she needed to be looking directly at a subject to magnify them in her vision. Mirrors only distorted the image when she tried to use them to zoom in.

"Soccer moms generally drive SUVs," Luka and Amirah burst out laughing at the irony. "But seriously, whoever is following us is probably a newbie or tagger."

"Tagger?" Amirah asked, looking at Luka, enjoying their newfound camaraderie.

"I believe both the HSA and PSI have them," Luka slowed down and switched to the inside lane until he came up on a side road and swung into it. "They are agents that do nothing but follow and collect information on their targets."

"Where are we going?" Amirah asked as Lukas tires spewed up dirt and stone on what seemed to be a farm road.

"Off-roading," His face lit up with a boyish grin. "Junction twelve is about four miles up ahead. This road wraps around, making it seem as if we are going in the opposite direction." He watched Amirah grab hold of the roof as he swung off the dirt road onto a track that seemed to wind up the mountainside.

"So, we are taking a long way around then?" she enquired as the pickup bumped across the terrain.

Luka handled the pickup as it sent a dust trail in its wake on the minor country road. "Nope, we are making sure that any taggers are slowed down and cannot access…" she nearly screamed when the car skidded around the vehicle and literally flew over a small ledge to bounce onto another tiny dirt road that looked more like a path than a road. "Good grief, you lunatic," Amirah punched Luka on the arm, feeling better at his small yelp.

"Relax. I know what I am doing and…"

They drove up a steep incline that showed junction twelve once they were car-bound over the top. "Junction twelve," he smiled, enjoying their off-roading adventure a little too much. "It will take the taggers time to figure out where we are headed."

They finally turned onto junction twelve. Luka could feel Amirah relaxed once they were on a nicely finished civilized road once again. "There are a few ways we could have gone from the first turnoff, and the tagger car would not have made it onto the first road."

"I cannot imagine why," Amirah breathed; she was still looking a bit green from their adventure through the countryside.

"So, why do you think whoever's scent in Josh's house is at Shellside Bay?" Luka asked, turning toward the small town.

"I never said we were going to Shellside Bay," Amirah looked at him suspiciously again, there were six towns along this route.

Luka put his hand beneath his seat and pulled out a photo he had taken from the lounge. He handed it to her and watched her eyes become teary again when she looked at it.

"Josh," she whispered, tracing his face before eyeing out the other man in the photo. Amirah grabbed her bag from her feet and fidgeted in it, pulling out a shirt.

"Did you steal that from the crime scene?" Luka asked her. "You know that is a crime, right?"

"Seriously?" Amirah held up the photo. "What about this?" she asked, her eyebrows shooting up questioningly before her brows furrowed in contemplation as something dawned on her. "You must have taken this photo from the house when we first got there because I don't recall seeing it." Her eyes searched his face, noting the clenching of his jaw. She looked back at the photo, the haircut, the way he stood could only mean one thing —the man was a hunter.

"Do you know this man?" Amirah held the photo up, pointing at the man with Josh. "Because his shirt was also in Josh's house." Amirah held up the shirt she had pulled out from her bag. It matched the one the man was wearing in the photo.

"I think it might be Quinton," Luka told her. "He was on my team back when I was with the PSI Special Unit."

Luka ran his hand through his hair as the dark churned inside him, that dark that stirred inside every time the nightmares or day terrors hit him. He gave a slight laugh, wondering how safe she would feel if she knew about the day terrors or why he was on "light duty" as his company so politely put it. He took a deep breath to get a grip over the dark, which was starting to overwhelm him, as he knew he owed her an explanation. If this was going to work, they needed some trust between them.

"Our last mission together turned into one I am not ready to discuss with anyone." He wanted to assure her it was not just her; he was not telling. "I thought Quinton was dead." He pulled the pickup over as his hands shook. He needed to concentrate on not going full psycho as he did whenever he talked about anyone from his unit or that day. "When I saw that photo at first, I thought it was someone who only looked like Quinton."

Luka took another deep breath, his knuckles turning white on the steering wheel as he fought to keep his cool. "I was shocked because I never knew Quinton was gay;

he had a fiancée." Luka pointed to a blue mark sticking out from Quinton's shirt sleeve on his bicep. "That is the lower part of our team's insignia. We all had tattooed on our arms after our first mission together."

~ ❤ ~

Amirah watched Luka struggling to control whatever demons were clawing at him from the inside. She did not need him to tell her what had happened on that fateful mission to know it had scarred him and left him branded for life. She could relate to what he was going through. She knew those demons only too well. She was mad at him for not trusting her with the truth, but something told her even if they were not headed for Shellside Bay, he would have shown her the photo when the time was right.

"So, I guess we both committed crimes today then," she smiled at him while keeping her voice soothing. She knew how to soothe a troubled mind and soul; it was one of her unique abilities. One she had had even before becoming a vampire.

He looked at her and gave a soft laugh, "I guess we are," he fidgeted in the inside pocket of his jacket. "But in full disclosure, I got you something else from the house." He pulled out a vial full of ash. "I was going to give this to you when we got back into the city, but I think now is a more appropriate time."

"Luka Brock, it looks like Sophie is not the only little thief everyone needs to look out for," Amirah laughed. Before she could check herself, she leaned over to give Luka a kiss on the cheek for the thoughtful felony he had committed for her. The moment her lips met his warm, slightly stubbled cheek, his rich scent wrapped itself around her. He turned his head towards her. Their eyes locked, and the world seemed to melt away. She swallowed as she could feel her heart pounded in anticipation. At the same time, a tinge of excitement set off a ripple of flutters in her stomach. Luka leaned in. As did she, only to be rudely stunned back to reality by a blaring horn.

Dazed, Amirah and Luka turned towards the car, trying to turn into the driveway they blocked. The man trying to get into the driveway was not thrilled and was flapping his arms, shouting at them to get a room. Well, he was shouting until his eyes met Luka's through their windshields. In an instant, the man's tanned face turned ashen. He sat wide-eyed for a few seconds before putting his car into reverse and speeding off. Their almost encounter still dazed Amirah and Luka as they sat and watched the car disappear into the distance before either could talk again.

"What the hell was that about?" Luka's question came out at the same time as Amirah's "That was rather odd."

They looked at each other, feeling the magnetic pull for a few seconds before both clearing their throats and looking forward. Both deciding to focus on that strange encounter instead of what had nearly happened between them.

~ ❤ ~

"Your clan member Josh really loved nice things," Luka whistled as they got out of the pickup truck at the house Josh and Quinton were standing in front of Shellside

Bay. In the driveway was a low-slung silver Maserati; it was recently driven as the engine was still warm as Luka found out by touching the hood. He looked at Amirah to show that there was someone in the house, but she already knew. Of course, she did! He grinned; it was nice to know you had a partner few people could sneak up on.

Amirah kept her senses on alert, listening for the sound of whoever was in the house. Luka indicated he would go around the back, leaving Amirah to go to the front door.

"Hello?" Amirah called, ringing the doorbell again and again. "Josh?" she called through the door. "Honey, it's me, Amirah. I know you are in there."

She could hear activity, but it was muffled. Before she could sink deeper into her senses, the door opened. Quinton stood there staring at her with the same look she was getting used to from Luka. It must be a hunter thing. Ice cold with a hint of warning laced with a touch of threat.

"Is Josh home?" Amirah asked Quinton, craning her neck to see inside his house. "I'm Amirah." She held out her hand for which she just got another cold hard stare.

"No, sorry, he is not," Quinton told her while he watched her suspiciously.

"But his car is in the driveway, and I really need to speak to him about urgent family matters." Amirah gave Quinton her most alluring smile that worked on all sexes, no matter their orientation.

She tried to push her way in, but Quinton stopped

her, not budging nor showing her any fear. Typical bloody hunter! Amirah thought, her eye catching a stealthy figure creeping up behind Quinton. "Look, I am asking you nicely to let me in," Amirah said patiently to the man.

"I told you that Josh is not here," Quinton said, standing his ground.

"Well, then, I guess we are going to do this the hard way."

Amirah slammed open the door as Luka expertly restrained Quinton from behind. He cut off his oxygen supply just enough to make Quinton pass out.

But it was not Quinton that dropped unconscious to the floor; it was Luka as a horrible resounding thud echoed through the room.

The minute the smell of fresh blood-filled Amirah's nostrils, she shoved a glazed Quinton out of the way like a rag doll and dived towards Luka lying on the floor for the count.

"Luka," she called to him, trying to find the wound on his head when a familiar voice said.

"He will be fine; just help me get him up onto the couch." Amirah's head shot up, and her heart felt like it would explode at the sight of Josh standing over Luka. Fire extinguisher in hand.

In a flash, Amirah stood up and had Josh in her arms, gripping him so tight he started complaining about not being able to breathe and moaning about her crushing a rib.

NINE

A Hard Truth

"YOU SCARED ME HALF TO DEATH!" AMIRAH MOANED AT Josh, while he and Quinton moved Luka to the couch. "I thought you had turned into a pile of ash." Amirah fished the vial Luka had given her out of her handbag.

"Did you get this from my house?" Josh asked her, his expression changing to one of fear.

"I did." Luka's deep voice came from the couch along with a wince. "What the hell did you hit me with?" He glared at Josh before saying, "If it is not you in there, then who is it?" Luka pushed himself to his feet and swayed. Three pairs of hands rushed to stop him from falling on his face. "I'm fine," he said through gritted teeth. "Although I could use some aspirin."

Quinton picked the bottle Josh had placed on the coffee table for Luka and handed them to him along with a glass of water. "It's good to see you, Quinton," Luka smiled at his long-lost teammate. "I thought you were dead."

Quinton looked at Luka blankly. "I'm sorry, but do I

know you?" Quinton asked Luka, eyeing him out as one did a complete stranger approaching them on the street.

Amirah and Luka's eyes met across the room. Hers looked worried while his eyes shone with confusion. "Do you remember the team?" Luka took off his jacket and rolled up his shirt sleeve to show Quinton their tattoos matched.

"What does it mean?" Quinton asked Luka looking at the tattoo that matched his.

"It is the insignia of the Special Forces team we were on."

"Luka was the commander," Amirah beamed, and then checked herself. Where had that come from? Heat flushed her cheeks in embarrassment as she felt like she was boasting about her quarterback boyfriend.

"I'm sorry, but I do not recall ever being in any Special Forces unit," Quinton told him before excusing himself on the guise of going to make everyone some coffee.

As he left, Luka moved so fast that Josh had no time to react. In a flash, he had Josh pinned to the wall in a death grip; no vampire could escape from "What have you done to him?" Luka hissed at a terrified Josh hanging a few feet off the floor. Josh was no light-weight either, which spoke volumes as to Luka's strength.

"Nothing," Josh swallowed around the death grip on his thorax, knowing one wrong move, and this hunter would not flinch from ripping his throat out. "Put me down, and I will explain."

"You will explain now," Luka growled; this entire day, he had felt like he had been chasing his tail. Like he was playing some game of cat and mouse while being led around by the nose. It was time for answers, starting with a vampire that was supposed to be a pile of ash.

"Put him down, Luka," Amirah commanded from behind him. "There is some logical explanation for this. Not even Josh can completely wipe someone's memory like that." Amirah pleaded for the life of her family member. "I can feel that these two would never hurt each other." Amirah watched, terrified, as Luka's fingers tightened around Josh's throat.

There was a distinct click of a gun being cocked, and a red dot spotted Luka's head.

"You heard the lady," Quinton's voice was soft and deadly. "Now put him down."

Amirah was not too happy with a gun pointed at Luka's head. Still, she was not too happy either with Luka's hand skillfully wrapped around Josh's Adam's apple. She watched relief flooding through her as Luka's hand around Josh's neck loosened.

"If I die, so does your boy toy here," Luka sneered at Quinton, his anger fueling the darkness inside of him. "Now, start talking." He lifted Josh a little higher to make his point.

Quinton, fearing for Josh's life, turned the gun on Amirah as he said in a cold flat voice, "I may not remember who I am, but I know I can put a bullet in her head before she can get to me."

Amirah turned and froze as the red light from Quinton's deadly looking gun was aimed at her head.

"Quinton, don't be an idiot," Josh admonished him. "I would never forgive you if you hurt Amirah." Josh looked at Luka, his eyes pleading now. "I have seen that look in his eyes, please. You have to save Amirah. I promise I will tell you everything I know." Luka saw the desperation in his eyes, and the red dot pointed at Amirah's head made him go cold.

What happened next happened so fast that even Amirah, with her super speed, would not have been able to stop it. Before Quinton, Josh, or Amirah knew what was happening, Luka had vaulted across the room and tackled Quinton. The gun went off, and Amirah was knocked to the ground by Josh as the chandelier crashed to the floor right where she had been standing.

That was it! There was just far too much testosterone in this room, and she had nearly gotten squashed by a chandelier. Amirah had had enough! She stood, her eyes getting huge as she watched Luka disarm Quinton before flinging him across the room like he was nothing more than a speck of lint. Quinton got up ready to counter-attack, only to be stopped by Amirah's piercing whistle. All three men grabbed their heads, nearly collapsing as the sound pierced through them.

That was weird. Amirah did not have a supersonic whistle, yet all three men buckled like she was a banshee. Cool! Did she just say cool? Amirah shuddered, one day with a hunter, and already she had picked up vulgar habits.

〜 〜 〜

"How is your head?" Amirah asked Luka as she sipped on a well-aged fine whiskey. She was still shell-shocked at the strength and speed of him.

"It's fine," Luka was being really short with her. In the past hour, she had gotten nothing but a few curtly worded answers from him, and he only spoke to her when she spoke to him.

"Where is Josh?" Luka looked at his watch "He should be back by now. I have waited long enough. If he is not back in ten minutes, we are going to look for him." Luka stood up from the couch and swayed. Damn head injury. He breathed through the pain and cool grey mist that kept wanting to draw him under. He reached down and picked up the bottle of aspirin, popping another four of them.

"Don't you think you have had enough of those?" Quinton asked from across the room, flinching when Luka turned to glare at him.

Quinton might be trained, and his body was combat-ready, but Luka was on another level altogether. In fact, Josh, Amirah, nor he had ever seen anything like the way Luka moved or the injuries he could sustain. He also recovered from an injury way too fast, especially a head wound. Anyone else would have had a severe concussion being knocked out so hard by a vampire.

"I think you should sit down," Amirah said. "Josh will come back soon. He went to fetch the takeout, which you know can take a bit of time, especially at this time of the evening."

"He is supposed to be dead. So, please tell me again why he was the one to go get the takeout?" Luka looked down at Amirah as if he was trying to see through her.

"I glamoured him," Amirah shrugged at the look of surprise on Luka's face. "It is easy to do."

"But it is something you can do?" Luka's eyes slit suspiciously at her. "Which means you have the power to impersonate anyone? And it is something you have not listed with the Paranormal Abilities Bureau for audit."

"Maybe they should have a Human Abilities

Bureau, and then you can register as a first-class dick," Quinton commented from across the room, smiling smugly at Luka's look. There was something oddly familiar about the guy, Quinton thought, familiar and safe.

"Quinton, please stop antagonizing our guest," Josh said as he entered the house, the smell of Chinese food filling the air and making all their stomachs rumble. Both Amirah and Luka had not eaten the entire day. And it had been a strange, emotionally charged, stressful day for them all.

Josh moved them all to the dining room, where they sat around the table, dishing up. Before he sat down, he picked up a small device saying, "Please, all turn off your mobile phones." Once all the phones were off and put in a weird-looking container, Josh pushed a button on the remote, explaining that it was a signal blocker. Amirah and Luka exchanged looks, each knowing the other both felt those now-all-too-familiar warning bells.

~ ~ ~

"I found Quinton wandering around Shellside Bay," Josh started, "He had a nasty infected looking wound above his eye and scratches on his neck."

"No." Quinton stopped Josh. "Tell them the truth." Quinton and Josh looked at each other. Josh's look clearly asked him if he was sure, but Quinton nodded.

"Fine," Josh could not understand why Quinton trusted this brute, but he did, and so did Amirah, apparently. "Quinton and I met eight months before his last mission."

"That would have been around April two years

ago," Luka said, giving Quinton a curious look that did not go amiss with Amirah.

"And a couple of months before you told me you were gay," Amirah remembered that day well. They had just shared a rather passionate afternoon together, so it did come as a surprise. Josh was the one man that if they were in need; they would seek each other out. He had taken that seductive photo of her posing on his yacht docked at the Shellside Bay yacht club where they had gone for dinner. That is when she had given him her mother's picture frame to put it in and keep beside him always.

"You are both correct," Josh said to them. "We fell in love, both not realizing it at first." Josh and Quinton smiled at each other. "They called Quinton away for work. I did not know what he did, only that it was something to do with the PSI."

Josh drew in a deep breath as he remembered the next part. "Three months turned into six months, and I had heard nothing from Quinton. I eventually called Grant for help; we had a brotherly heart-to-heart talk, and he found out for me what had happened to him." Josh's hand shook as he lifted his wine glass. "Quinton was presumed dead in a raid that was carried out by a rather vicious faction."

"What?" Luka's head snapped around towards Josh. "Quinton was with me on a mission to infiltrate a vampire coven." Luka gripped the table, his knuckles turning white as he fought for control, swatting back the heinous memories of that mission.

"No, Luka, he was not," Josh said softly. Josh watched Luka wearily. "Neither were you."

Shock zinged through Luka at what Josh had just

said, making him wonder why he had not ripped this lying vampire's throat out.

"You're lying," Luka hissed warningly at Josh. "I remember that entire mission as plain as day. I live it, breathe it, sweat it, and fear it every day." Emotion rasped through Luka, the vein on his neck throbbed erratically as the anger bubbled inside him again. "Every night I hear the screams of my men being torn apart, I can smell their death staining my conscience."

"No, he is not lying," Quinton said calmly. His stance telling Luka he was ready to go another round should Luka get hostile again.

"I don't understand," Amirah piped in to give Luka a chance to calm down. "Luka was responsible for taking down Bronlynn's coven of vampires in November of that year." It was the information she had got when she was researching Luka only yesterday.

"Yes, they did," Josh said. "Only Bronlynn's coven was not the original target." Josh watched Luka's shoulders stiffen, his brow creased into a frown before he closed his eyes. "Luka!" Josh banged on the table. He could not let Luka remember everything right now, especially if he reacted as Quinton had. And Luka was a lot faster and a heck of a lot stronger than Quinton. Josh had never seen a human move quite as Luka did. And Luka was one hundred percent human, well, at least according to the rather impressive PSI file he was.

"Your original mission was to take down a rather nasty faction made up of paranormals, humans, and other vile creatures. Most of which are the likes that humans and most paranormals do not know actually exist." Josh took another sip of his drink. "The operation went sideways, and most of your team ended up slaughtered."

Josh watched the haunting look that glazed Luka's eyes. He had seen it many times in Quinton's before they had suppressed his memories. "The faction captured the rest. This included you, Quinton..." Josh looked over at Amirah; he knew she did not know this, but continued, "Morgan, and four others we have not found yet."

"Morgan?" Amirah and Luka said in unison, their eyes locked together in shock.

"Yes, Amirah," Josh placed his hand over hers. "He volunteered on this mission. The PSI and HSA were joining forces to take down factions such as these that are springing up all over the world." Josh watched as Amirah and Luka absorbed all the information Josh was telling them.

Luka did not want to believe him, but deep down, he knew what Josh was saying was true. There were many nights that certain aspects of the mission made little sense to Luka. He could never quite figure out how the coven had got a drop on his team or how they had brutally attacked them as they did. The research he had secretly been doing on Bronlynn's coven revealed they were also made up of humans and paranormals. But they took in abused women, children, and even men. They were a shelter for anyone who needed it. The more he researched the coven, the more the images of how they had been slaughtered and left as an example haunted him, along with the fact that he and his team had killed a movement trying to set things right in the world. It now also began to make sense as to why all

Morgan's records had disappeared and maybe why he had been turned to ash.

"Morgan?" Amirah was in shock; she knew Morgan was a brilliant scientist working on cures for various diseases. She never once suspected he was an HSA field agent or that he went on dangerous missions. Confusion spun around her mind as she said, "Morgan is dead, Josh. I tried to call you, but you were not answering." Her mind spun. This was too much. It had been a weird day and was only getting weirder, not to mention more complicated by the minute. What the hell was her clan mixed up in? And how the hell had she got caught up in all this?

"Are you okay?" Luka's deep voice brought her out of her panic; she smiled at him and nodded before taking a huge swallow of the red wine in her glass, then topping it up.

"I am sorry about Morgan. He was a wonderful brother," Josh told her softly. "But you need to know the rest because all our lives are in danger."

"Why are we all in danger?" Luka asked, looking at Josh with the same look he did when he pinned him against the wall a few hours ago.

"That is what I am trying to figure out and probably why I now have a target on my back." Josh saluted them and took a sip of his wine. "We will get back to the target on my back part, but I need to explain about Quinton."

"The thing about that mission was, your team was deployed in November, but the Bronlynn coven mission happened almost twelve weeks after you were deployed," Josh watched Luka stiffen.

"That is because we were captured. One of the

covens had managed to get close to us because of an association with one of the team members." Luka fought to keep from getting lost in those memories again. "I was able to get loose, and we managed to escape and complete the mission, taking the coven by surprise." Luka's jaw clenched as he held back the images and the guilt that they now brought, a pang of guilt which had intensified as Josh confirmed his findings.

"No, Luka, you were not captured by Bronlynn's coven." Josh watched the emotions flicker in Luka's eyes and knew that he was only confirming what he felt Luka already suspected. "You were captured by the Rites of Adam."

"The Rites of Adam?" Amirah questioned. "Are you sure?" Her skin began to crawl. That scent she had picked up in the air at Josh's house came back to her. Impossible. Amirah thought to try to mask her fear from the men in the room.

"Yes, I am sure." Josh knew both Amirah and Luka were not going to like what was coming next. "Your mission was a bust because I am almost certain that high ranking members of both the HSA and PSI are also members of the Rites of Adam."

"No way," Luka instantly defended his agency; he had been with them since he was a nineteen-year-old misfit floating around from foster home to foster him until he no longer qualified for state care. General Trent had found him, given him a purpose, and helped him get back his life sorted out. "If there are, I will weed them out and deliver them to General Trent myself."

"We are not sure which ones or how high up it goes," Josh told him. "All I do know right now is that the

HSA and PSI were taken over by a new government agency yesterday. Your last mission, I believe, was the start of that amalgamation, when they added paranormals to your unit."

"No," Luka denied. "We were working together because of the abilities two of the vampires had that were useful to the mission." Although Luka could not for the life of him remember what those were or who the vampires were.

"Luka, they used your botched mission as an excuse to disband the special elite team. Your team," Josh said. "It gave the powers that be the ammunition they needed to create the PSI from the World Paranormal and Mystical Regulations Bureau."

Luka stared at Josh in disbelief; he really wanted to dispute everything the vampire said, but deep down, he knew it to be true. He had known for a long time that there was something amiss with the PSI.

"Grant," Amirah's said from out of nowhere as a thought hit her. Her eyes searched Josh's eyes, looking for confirmation that he was not involved in any of this.

"I can't say for sure," Josh answered her without her asking. "But I can tell you he has been involved in some off the book's scientific research amalgamation projects with the HSA and PSI for the past four to five years." He hated having to tell her, but she needed to know that she could trust no one outside of this room. He still did not fully trust Luka and had to keep Quinton mesmerized until they could work through his memories.

"When you, and what was left of your team, returned from that final mission, the agency had you all in lock-down in one of their military-grade medical facilities," Josh continued. "You were there for over six months." As his words echoed across the table, he knew that Luka's memories were untangling the truth from what the agency had drummed into him. Josh put his hand beneath the table and closed it around the tranquilizer gun he had there. He was not sure how Luka would react when his actual memories surfaced, and he was not going to get caught off guard if it was anything like the way Quinton had.

"Quinton found his way back to me. But he was not the same. He would wake up at night screaming, he even had day terrors where he would slip into some sort of trance. He tried to kill me a few times until one day; he could not take it anymore." Josh's eyes filled with tears as he watched Quinton smile at him, pull out his phone, fiddle with it, and push it towards Luka.

Luka looked down at it; it was a video of Quinton. He clicked play:

"My name is Quinton Banyon Banks. I am an elite officer of the PSI Special Forces.

I have asked Josh O'Connell to mesmerize me until I can control what is happening to me. I recently returned from a mission that went horribly wrong; we were captured, tortured, and misled. We wrongfully attacked a coven, slaughtering innocents, one of which was my sister, Jackie Banks."

Luka's head shot up, the memory clear as day of Jackie tending to Quinton's wounds. "You. It was you that had the association with the coven."

Luka looked at Quinton; his eyes were filled with tears of guilt and anguish.

$\smile \,\smile\,\smile$

"Are you sure it was them you saw in Shellside Bay?" the general asked the man on the other side of the phone.

"Yes," the reply from the other end of the phone was a desperate plea for help.

"Don't worry; I am sure you were not recognized." The general called one of the officers who had been called to the general's office. "I will send a team to get you, hang tight." When the conversation ended, the general turned to the officer.

"Our good doctor needs extraction," the general informed the officer. "Make sure it is done efficiently and that there is nothing that can be traced back to us." The officer nodded and saluted, "We don't want to reveal our hand just yet." A smile spread across the general face at the delicious thought of how close they were to accomplish their goal.

TEN

No Denying Desire

IT HAD BEEN A CRAZY DAY; LUKA HAD GONE INTO WAR with otherworldly creatures and stood toe with paranormal beings that could melt a person's mind. But today had been a day like no other he could remember.

Luka's head pounded where that lunatic Josh had whacked him. It had been too late to head back to the city, so Amirah and Luka stayed the night in Shellside Bay. He got up and softly padded to the lounge in search of the aspirin.

"I see you can't sleep either," Amirah's soft voice floated to him as she shone a torch towards where he stood. He turned, froze, balled his hands in fists at his sides, and battled to control his libido that had sprung into action the moment he had sensed her coming down the hallway.

He swallowed, his throat suddenly dry. "My head was throbbing, so I came in search of these," he held up the pill bottle before walking into the dark kitchen to grab a glass of water.

"You should get that looked at when we are back in the city," Amirah said with concern.

"Maybe," he smiled, finishing the glass of water, watching her move closer towards him. Her satin robe was loosely belted at the waist, but when she walked, it fell open, offering him a glimpse of her long, naked legs.

"Let me take a look," she stopped in front of him, a small flashlight in her hands. "You will have to bend your head a little." He obliged, dipping his head forward. Her fingers ran through his hair, gently probing around for any damage until he winced when her fingers touched the bump. "That is a large bump," she whispered, and without thinking, she leaned forward and touched her lips to it. She felt him shudder and heard him suck in a breath as he rasped.

"It feels much better," his voice was soft and gruff. He turned towards her; they were standing so close they could feel the heat from each other's bodies. Their eyes locked in the low torchlight as their lips drew closer together, their breathing became more labored. Once again, the world around them faded away until their lips touched. His mind reeled as the heat consumed his body; he pulled away slightly, trying not to lose control. Then she licked her lips, and he could no longer resist the pull; his lips crushed hers. Amirah wrapped her arms around his neck as he lifted her so she could wrap her legs around him. They turned, and he moved her to the counter, their passion deepening as their kisses grew steamier. Her hands roamed down her back until they found the hem of his shirt, and she pulled it up. Her hands found his flesh and traced the muscles of his back. He needed to get closer to her; he wanted to feel her skin against his. He slid her gown down over her shoulders, his lips following the path of his hands.

A sound from the bathroom caught their attention, drawing them apart. Amirah fixed her gown while Luka poured himself some water and downed it. His body shook with the impact of being close to her. Never had he been so hungry for someone in all his life. He downed another glass of water, battling against the desire to turn around and lose himself in her.

Amirah felt as if her world was spinning around her like she had lost a part of her skin when Luka drew away from her. Her entire body shook with a deep need for him, one she could honestly say she had never felt before. Amirah drew in a deep mental breath, willing herself to get a grip. She had been around for a long time, and this was not her first kiss. Although oddly enough, it had felt… No, Amirah, you are just being an idiot with a weird crush! Hell, she was being the type of woman that she tried to warn her female clients not to be.

She hopped off the counter, glad that Luka's back was turned as she nearly collapsed. Her legs felt like jelly.

"Well, I'm…" Luka turned around to look at her, his eyes were still dark with desire. Amirah swallowed hard, fighting against every instinct in her body that wanted to meld her lips with his and melt into him. Amirah gave her head a mental shake; well, she hoped she gave her head a mental shake. Right now, she was not thinking clearly; her brain felt like fuzz. Her body was trying to rebel against her brain, especially when he looked at her the way he was looking at her. The raw desire in his eyes made her cold heart pound in her chest while the heady scent of his need was like invisible arms pulling her in. But she could sense he too was battling against whatever this was between them.

A goodnight was all Amirah said before turning and going back to her room. She closed the door, allowing herself to collapse against it and slide down to the cool tiled floor. The shock of the icy floor could not even stop this fire that was raging through her blood. Never could Amirah remember a time she had wanted any man this badly, so why Luka? Maybe it was because it was forbidden and because she knew she could not have him, so she wanted him more. Or maybe it was the challenge of bending an alpha male such as him to her will —yes that was it. The only reason she wanted Luka like this was that he was such a challenge. That made her feel better and explained the overpowering desire she had for him. She stood up from the icy floor and padded over to her bed, ignoring the other small voice in her head.

They were heading back to the city early as Amirah had to get back to work. Luka needed to assimilate the information Josh had given him. He was still reeling from what he had been told, finding Quinton as well as Josh alive. Josh knew he had a target on his back when a druid, who also turned out to be one of Amirah's vampire clan, arrived with a blood sample he had ordered to track with. Only Josh had not ordered anything from the HSA. Within a few minutes of the Druid entering his house, the Druid collapsed on the floor. Josh noticed blood pooling on the floor and had to draw back the Druid's hood. It was Humphrey, a young wizard Amirah had turned a few years after she had turned Josh. It was not long after that Humphrey turned to ash. It was a warning and a frame-up. So Josh and Quinton fled, taking the Druid's vial of blood with them. The blood in the vial turned out to be Quinton's. It did not look good for Josh as the druids would know he was not dead and would now assume he had killed Humphrey. To the druids, HSA, and PSI, Josh may as well have launched an attack on Switzerland.

There was this uncomfortable silence in the car. He and Amirah had not said a lot since their encounter last night. They needed to work together, so he knew he had to clear the air.

"Amirah, about last night," his voice caught as their image flashed through his head. He cleared his throat. "I apologize; it was unprofessional of me, and I promise it won't happen again. I would like to blame the concussion, but the fact is you are one of the most incredible women I have ever known." He swallowed and fought the temptation to stop the pickup and crush his lips to her. What was the matter with him? His knuckle whitened on the steering wheel. "I admit I am so attracted to you. But we can never happen as I am sure you are aware. Besides, I know how much you loathe my type." He smiled; trying to lighten the tension that he could feel was building in the car again.

He turned to look at her, expecting to see... well, he never knew what to expect from her. She continually surprised him and kept him on his toes. She was looking at him with an expression he could only think was shock.

~ ~ ~

"I was not expecting that," Amirah told him once her shock and surprise wore off enough for her to realize she was gaping at him. She never gaped at anyone. When he had started to talk about what happened last night, Amirah felt sure he would give her the "it is not you, it is me" speech. Instead, he once again knocked her off guard with total honesty.

"You keep surprising me, Luka Brock," Amirah smiled at him, secretly wondering if she could compel him to forget her open mouth moment of shock. She was sure it was not a pleasant look for anyone. "I agree with you and was thinking along the same lines."

They pulled into the car park of Luka's apartment building. As Amirah got out of the pickup, she said, "If you want to talk to my clients, you should come to the mixer on Saturday night."

"I'm not a single-mingle type guy, but I guess it will give us a chance to check out your clients."

"No, I meant for you to ask them 'if I am sampling my clients. I think that is how you put it?"

"I thought we were past that," Luka quipped. "I no longer think you would do something like that. I thought that was implied when we teamed up on our adventure."

Once again, Luka had surprised her, and again, Amirah did not know quite what to say until something else he had said dawned on her, spoiling the moment.

"Wait a minute...," Amirah's eye slit in on him.

"You now think one of my clients might be involved in all of this."

"Yes, I thought that was implied when we all agreed that everyone other than the four of us could be trusted." Luka held the lift open for her.

"You know, just when I think you are not who I thought you were..." she shook her head in exasperation.

She was so irritated she tripped, and Luka reached out, stopping her from falling by pulling her up against him. Her hands were flat against his chest; she lifted her head to look up at him. His eyes darkened with that hunger she had seen in them last night, she felt her pulse quicken and could not stop herself from dragging his head down to crush his lips against hers.

~ ~ ~

Luka did not remember pushing the button for his apartment, nor did he remember getting to the front door. All he remembered was the desire burning through him with a force the likes he had never felt before. All his brain and body could concentrate on was Amirah; he knew he had to have her then and there, to hell with protocol and everything else. Luka could remember the feel of her soft lips, smooth satin skin, tantalizing scent, and her oh so talented fingers.

~ ~ ~

Amirah let herself into her apartment. She felt like a giddy school girl; she walked to her window to see Luka standing there watching her. She zoomed in and laughed; he held up a picture of a smiley face blowing a kiss at her. Amirah drew one back, pulled out the phone Sophie had given her, and sent him a sexy message, laughing at the one he sent back. She watched as he turned away from the window, and for the first time ever in her very long life, she felt annoyed that she had to go to work. She could have spent the entire day or more lying in Luka's arms.

ELEVEN

Finding Luka

AMIRAH HAD NOT HEARD A PEEP OUT OF LUKA FOR TWO days now. She had to keep herself from asking Rachel every few minutes if he had RSVP'd to the invitation she had sent him to the mixer. His apartment had been dark since the day they had gotten back from Shellside Bay. It was nice that no one had turned to ash or no one she knew of in the past two days, and she hated herself for wanting someone to just, so she had an excuse to see him again.

Something pricked her ears, an altercation at Rachel's desk; she tuned her ears in. "Look, just push that little button there and let Amirah know that I am here to see her." Amirah's heart skipped a beat. Was Luka with her? Then her heart sank. Wait, why was Sophie here? Had something happened to Luka?

"Amirah is busy at the moment, and you do not have an appointment. Can you not read?" Amirah swung her office door open to see an almost familiar scene replaying itself between Rachel and Sophie. Amirah smiled as she saw Rachel pointing to the letters on the door.

"Listen, prissy missy, my IQ is higher than you can probably count to," Sophie sneered back at Rachel. "I know this may be hard for you to do, considering you probably still have a few years training to do, but here, let me speed things up and push the button for you." Sophie pulled herself up on Rachel's desk, ready to hit the intercom as Rachel's hand shot over and grabbed Sophie's.

"Where are all you PSI agents raised? In a barn like farm animals?" Rachel held onto Sophie's arm, who was slapping at her hand.

"Okay, ladies, break it up!" Amirah walked over to where the two young women were having a hand-slapping match and pushed them apart.

"She started it," Sophie said, pointing to Rachel, who made a face at her.

"You and your Neanderthal colleague need to learn some manners and how to read!" Rachel sneered at Sophie.

"Hey, that is enough," Amirah wanted to laugh. So, this is what it must be like having two teenage daughters. "You," Amirah pointed at Rachel, "back to work; there is still a lot to do for the function on Saturday." Amirah gently steered Sophie into her office, saying, "You come with me." The making a face did not go unnoticed by Amirah, who was trying really hard not to laugh.

"Love the office," Sophie twirled around Amirah's super modern and sleek executive office. "Oh, my hat."

Sophie ran to the floor to ceiling window to stare at the view. "Wow, how do you get any work done? I would stare at this the entire day."

Amirah watched Sophie skitter around her office like a puppy having to check out its new surroundings.

"I'm glad you like my office, Sophie," Amirah smiled at the young woman. "But may I ask, what brings you here?" Sophie stopped her tour of Amirah's office, her face becoming serious. Once again, Amirah's heart plummeted. It was about Luka, and it was not good news because of the look on the girl's face.

"Have you heard from Luka?" Sophie looked Amirah dead in the eyes, making her flinch. That look was a complete change from the boisterous young girl who had just bounded around her office. In fact, it was a little scary. There was a lot more to Sophie than Amirah realized.

"No," Amirah told her.

"When last did you hear from or see him?" Sophie asked, and then stopped Amirah from talking as she took a strange-looking device from the satchel she had slung over her shoulder. Amirah watched as Sophie put it on the desk and flicked on the button. The device made no sound, but four amber lights blinked wildly.

Amirah was about to say something, but Sophie held her up and shook her head, indicating to Amirah not to say a word. The girl pulled out another small computer looking device, punched in a few keys before smiling and looking back up at Amirah saying. "Your office is totally bugged, and it was not done by me." Sophie pulled out two candy bars from her bag, offering one to Amirah, who declined. "I would love to say it is that dodo at your front desk, but I doubt she can even download an app on her phone." Sophie got stuck into her candy bar before continuing. "So, you were about to tell me when last you saw or heard from Luka." Sophie smiled at Amirah.

This girl perplexed Amirah, and she wondered if this is what ADHD looked like. "Is it okay to talk now?" Amirah asked Sophie.

"Oh, yes, sorry, I thought that was implied when I started talking again," Sophie laughed.

Amirah looked at the young girl in front of her, no older than nineteen, twenty at the most. She held up a brave front, but Amirah could tell she was also scared, worried, and tired. Amirah frowned at Sophie, looking at the girl more closely. "When last did you sleep, Sophie?" Amirah asked her.

"Not since Luka got back from his final mission with the elite force," Sophie told her, looking Amirah in the eye. Her gaze was wary and had a hint of street smarts that said she could more than handle nearly anything.

"I last saw Luka two days ago when he dropped me off from Josh's house," Amirah informed the girl; it was not exactly a lie.

"I want to believe you, Amirah, because everything I know about you indicates that you not only turned your life around but have helped lots of people regardless of species or sex," Sophie's eyes probed Amirah's. "But Luka went missing right after the bounty went out on your head for killing doctor Fuller."

"Who is Doctor Fuller?" Amirah looked at the young woman questioningly.

"He was the man who apparently beat up his wife very badly a month ago," Sophie turned her laptop around for Amirah to see. "His wife was Janet Fuller, one of the members of a support group for empowering women that you are listed as an avid supporter of."

Amirah went cold when she saw the PSI docket commanding action be taken against her as a hostile paranormal. "I didn't kill anyone," Amirah told the girl stunned.

"Is this you?" Sophie clicked up a video feed of a woman brutally attacking a man.

"No," Amirah told Sophie, her mind spinning.

Sophie zoomed in as the woman on the video turned to leave the man beaten and not moving. The woman in the hoodie looked up and down the street, before slinking off into the night. Amirah gasped, when Sophie zoomed in on the face, it was clearly her face.

"No," Amirah said she had not done anything like that. She had no knowledge of Janet Fuller or that particular support group.

"I will phone the HSA and get them to sort this out with the PSI," Amirah's hands shook as she picked up the phone to dial.

Sophie stopped her, "It was the HSA that ordered the hit to the PSI who assigned it to Luka two days ago."

Amirah's eyes grew wide. Now she was being framed for murder and the disappearance of Luka? Is that what Sophie was telling her?

"Sophie, I swear to you that is not me on that video." She glanced down and noted the time stamp. "I was not even in the city when that video was taken."

"I know," Sophie said, sitting back watching Amirah's look at her in astonishment.

"You know?" She asked Sophie, annoyed at the girl for making her feel like a suspect.

"Yes, I had you, and Luka bugged. The one you

found in the glove compartment, that was mine, not the PSIs," she pointed to the phone on Amirah's desk. "I knew by your GPS location on the phones I gave you that you were in Shellside Bay with Josh." She smiled at Amirah's shocked look. "Who do you think was navigating for the tracker in the white Prius?" Sophie looked at Amirah, frowning. "I had to make sure," her voice dropped.

Amirah smiled at the young woman, but then thoughts of Luka came back to her, and she said softly, "Luka has not been at his apartment."

"The day you got back from Shellside Bay, Luka was given the orders to bring you in at all costs," Sophie told her. "As soon as he left the office, he called me and told me to get everything I could, then leave." Sophie's voice dropped. "The agency was stormed by men I had never seen before. Jeff helped me to escape but was shot before he could."

"Oh, Sophie. I am so sorry," Amirah watched the young women fidgeting with her gadgets.

"Luka told me to meet him where we watched the stars. But he did not come, and then I found this," Sophie pulled up her laptop again and opened another PSI order. "This came in two hours after the building was stormed."

The docket read:

Order for the capture of Luka Brock. He is to be restrained but treated as extremely hostile and dangerous (code red).

"Luka!" Amirah whispered, fear clawing at her. "What is this all about, Sophie?" Amirah asked her, feeling helpless and so angry.

"I don't know, but what I do know is that there is a

team of HSA and PSI agents headed this way, and we need to get out of here as fast as we can."

Amirah grabbed up her things as did Sophie, who said, "You are going to have to bring the dodo with you." Amirah shook her head at Sophie's reference to Rachel.

~ ~ ~

"Where are we going and what is going on?" Rachel fumed as she hobbled on shoes that Amirah had broken the heels off of.

"Hush, prissy, missy," Sophie told her as she scanned a parking lot with a weird device. "Okay, we are headed into that parking lot over there."

They rushed towards the parking lot, trying to look as normal as possible.

"Shotgun," Sophie called as she popped up next to a white Prius.

"Really?" Amirah said disgustedly as she looked at the car. "A tagger car?"

"What is a tagger car?" Rachel asked, only to be ignored as Sophie looked questioningly at Amirah.

"What?" she looked at the car Amirah stood next to. "Oh no, not that thing." She clicked the remote she held in her hand, and the copper Land Cruiser behind her tweeted. "This is our vehicle." She smiled at the relief on Amirah's face before throwing her the keys and hauling herself into the passenger seat.

"You don't want to drive?" Amirah asked Sophie, climbing into the driver's seat. The car still had that new car smell about it. "This car is brand new."

"Nope, I'm not allowed to drive yet," Sophie told

her. "At least not with passengers, I don't really like to drive after Luka, and I had an accident when I was younger." Sophie smiled sadly as she looked around the interior. "And yes, it is new; I got it two weeks ago."

"Oh, did you buy it?" Amirah asked as they pulled out of the parking lot.

"No, it was a gift," Sophie told Amirah, busying herself with a device attached to her phone. "Luka bought it for me to encourage me to learn to drive. I think he is tired of playing Uber."

"My phone has not worked since Luka, and I went to Josh's house," Amirah told Sophie, "The phone company says there is nothing wrong with it."

"Can I have a look at it?" Sophie asked Amirah, who fished the device out of her pocket and handed it to the girl. Sophie looked at it, turned to Rachel, asking, "Can I see your phone, please?"

Rachel eyed Sophie suspiciously but handed it over, regretting it as soon as she did because Sophie opened the car window and flung both phones out. "There, that is much better."

"What the hell?" Rachel shouted, watching her phone bounce off the sidewalk and shattering behind them.

"Here, you can use these," Sophie gave them each a replica of the phones she got rid of. "Oh, and I downloaded a newer version of Candy Crush for you." She smiled sweetly at Rachel, who made a face at her.

"We need to get to the place Luka told me to meet him," Sophie punched in the coordinates on Amirah's new phone.

"So, now does anyone want to fill me in on WHAT THE HELL HAS BEEN GOING ON?" Rachel asked from the back seat, turning down the sound of Candy Crush she was playing.

"He is waking up."

Images blurred all around him as he tried to open his eyes further. He had a feeling someone was trying to reach him, calling out to him, or maybe it was just a crazy dream? He was just so tired, his body felt weak and so heavy. He was battling to keep his eyelids open.

"Hey there," an ugly, distorted face popped into his line of sight. "Now, it is not time for you to wake up, so I am more than happy to say this will hurt you a lot more than it is me."

Something stung his neck, the burning sensation that followed it made him feel like he had been injected with fire. Anger started to boil in his gut; he was about to tell the grotesque creature that he was going to break its neck. But as the fire cooled, a grey mist swirled up from the depth of his mind and started to drag him back to the darkness. The last thing he heard was a weird laugh as the creature waved, saying, "Night-night."

TWELVE

The Mad Man

As they left the city, Amirah's phone rang. It was a blocked number, and all three pairs of eyes settled on the phone. "Hello?" Amirah answered on speakerphone.

"Hello, Amirah," a weird simulated voice filled the car.

"Who is this?" Amirah asked; her senses going on high alert as her ears scanned for trace sounds on the other end of the line.

"You will find out soon enough," the voice laughed. "Did you like the video we made for you?" Another laugh before the voice told her. "Did it remind you of your blood reign days?" The voice taunted her, but she refused to take the bait. "Your boyfriend and some of your clan vampires are becoming a real nuisance."

"Again, I will ask you before I hang up, who is this?" Amirah was getting really frustrated as all background noise was drowned out.

"Like I said, you will find out soon enough," the voice told her confidently.

"Okay then, I am going to hang up," she was about to press the red button when a live image of Quinton, Josh, and Luka popped up on her screen. They were tied up and unconscious, but she could hear their heartbeats, so she knew they were alive. Before she could hear anything else, there was nothing but silence again as the voice came back on the line.

"I have three little piggies," the voice told her. "And guess what? The big evil wolf spiked their blood. So now the little piggies don't have long to live." The voice showed her a picture of a pile of ash on the floor.

"What do you want?" she breathed, her heart all but stopping at what the voice had just said.

"Go to the gas station about two miles from your current location. There is a surprise for you and the girls. You will get further instructions from there." Before the line went dead, the voice said to Sophie, "Nice try, Little Butterfly, but I always know where you are!"

"No," Sophie's eyes were huge, and Amirah could hear the girl's heartbeat racing in fear.

"Did that mean something to you?" Amirah asked her.

"About five months ago, I was being stalked by this deranged vampire of some faction," Sophie told Amirah, who was surprised by the weird outburst from Rachel, as she shouted.

"What?" Sophie gave Rachel a weird look and shook her head.

Amirah looked at the two girls; something else was going on here, but Sophie drew her attention back to what had happened to her.

"Luka called in some favors, and it was all sorted

out. I thought the stalker had been captured by the PSI. I thought they had the crazy vampire locked up." Sophie swallowed as she remembered that horrible time. Thank goodness Luka's house was a fortress. "The mad stalker was also a hacker that found out my hacker name is Little Butterfly."

Anger burned in Amirah's veins at how some people just thought they had a right to make someone else's life hell.

"He also threatened to kill Luka but that he would first make sure he lost everything he loved," Sophie's eyes looked up at Amirah's. They were filled with unshed tears and fear. "Now he has Luka."

"I am so sorry, Soph," Rachel whispered, her eyes filled with tears as she reached for Sophie's hand.

"Listen to me," Amirah said as she turned into the gas station. "This is not your fault, and we will find this lunatic. Do you hear me?"

Sophie nodded and wiped the tears that had spilled onto her cheeks away.

"Is that Luka's pickup?" Amirah asked Sophie, who nodded in confirmation, bolting out of the SUV as it drew to a stop.

As Sophie ran to the pickup with Amirah hot on her heels, they could see someone in the car.

"Luka, Luka," Sophie called, but as soon as they opened the door, the body disintegrated into ash. "Noooooo!" Sophie screamed her hands, trying desperately to catch and somehow put the ash back together. Turning to Amirah, with tears streaming down her cheeks again. "Amirah, please, please, help me."

Sophie piled ash into Amirah's hands, begging her to put him back together. Amirah stood horrified, her heart feeling like someone had put a knife through it. The ash flowed through her fingers while all she could do was stand there, staring at it in shock.

Something solid hit her palm; she looked down at the object caked with ash. She dusted off the ash to reveal a ring with an insignia she recognized on it. She closed her eyes, swallowing hard. She did not know which was worse as she scented the ring, gently stopping Sophie from trying to resurrect Luka from the ashes.

"It was not Luka in the pickup, Soph," Amirah gave Sophie the ring that had fallen through the ash. "There is no trace of Luka on that ring, only its owner." Amirah's eyes filled with tears. It might not have been Luka's, but it had been another clan vampire of hers. "I know because I know that scent well. It belongs to Daniel, one of my oldest and dearest clan vampires."

Relief flooded Sophie, but then so did sorrow. "Oh no, Amirah, I am so sorry," she started to gather up the ash she had thrown all over the place when she noticed a weird feeling from it. It had an oily residue. "Impossible." Sophie said, looking at her fingers then rushing off to get a clean evidence bag from her bag, she gathered up the ash.

"What is it?" Amirah asked Sophie, glad of the distraction.

"I think I know what is being used for the poison that did this."

"Slushy?" Rachel asked them. She was holding three big gulps filled with blue iced sugar slush. "They are giving them away as a free promotion." Rachel indicated the table by the gas station door.

"No, thank you," Amirah made a face. "That stuff will kill you."

"Oh yes, please," Sophie took one and slurped like she had just gone to heaven. "You have got to love bubblegum flavored crushed ice." She slurped again, asking Rachel, "Did you get anything to eat? I'm starving."

Amirah's phone rang. It was the blocked number. All three pairs of eyes looked at it. Amirah gave the girls some money to go get some snacks. "I will deal with this while you two go get something for the road." Amirah answered the call while she walked back to the SUV and pictured the many ways she was going to kill this freak when she found him. "Where are Luka, Josh, and Quinton?"

"I see you got the present we left you," he laughed; there was something so familiar about his laugh. "They are all still breathing, for now, that is."

"What do you want?" Amirah's anger breathed through the receiver.

"We want the Stone of Zara."

Amirah went cold, her face paling. "I don't know what you are talking about?"

"Well then, Amirah let me jog your memory for you." The voice said, "In about six minutes, your little band of young butterflies are going to become horribly sick. Those girls really should cut down on their sugary drinks." He laughed again, making Amirah want to hurl her phone across the parking lot. Instead, she ran up to the girls walking out of the store loaded with snacks and slushy refills. With a swoop of her hand, she knocked the big gulps out of the girls' hands.

"Stop drinking that." They looked at her in shock.

"Hey…" Sophie said. "I was drinking that."

"I'm afraid your parenting skills still leave a lot to be desired there, Amirah," the voice laughed, making Amirah go cold. Was the voice one of her clan vampires?

"Now, if you don't want those young ladies' deaths on your hands, you will need the antidote," the voice told her. "Just like your friends stuck here with me, do. So, now do you remember the Stone of Zara?" the voice asked.

"How do I know you have an antidote?" She asked him, "Or how do I know you have actually given them anything?"

"Are you willing to take that chance?" The voice asked, laughing, "I never took you for a gambling person, Amirah." That laugh again. "Okay, well, about now, the girls will either get a nose bleed or ear bleed. Depending on how their system reacts to the poison."

Amirah's face whitened as Rachel's ear started to bleed, as did Sophie's nose.

"What the…" Sophie said her eyes flying up to watch as Rachel grabbed her ear, crying out in pain while blood seeped through her fingers.

"Well, Amirah, you have about five minutes to decide what it will be and find out just how fast your vampire speed is as the shop assistant has your cure." The voice laughed, and before he hung up, said, "Oh, and while you are in there, could you please take care of a staffing problem for us? The shop assistant's services are no longer required."

"You bastard," Amirah hissed. She put the girls into the SUV, saying, "Don't move. I think you ingested some poison."

Amirah zipped into the shop. There was a lot of crashing and screaming, but she was back in a flash with two small vials.

"Drink these," Amirah popped the tops of each of them for the two women. She noticed their blood had a weird smell. It was not like Morgan's had smelled theirs reeked really sweet like they had ketones. But there was another weird scent in their blood? And that is when she heard it. Ever so slightly, but it was there. She had heard it earlier when they first got into the SUV. Was there a stow-away in the car? She scanned it, but there was nothing. Amirah shrugged it off and went back to attending to the girls.

"What was that?" Sophie asked as her bleeding nose stopped. The terrible burning pain in her stomach subsided after drinking the stuff in the vial. "Was that blood I just drank?" Sophie asked instantly, trying to wipe any leftover serum from her blue tongue before another cramp hit her stomach. "I will never drink slushy's again. Never ever again!" She muttered, leaning out the car and vomiting. "I think I need to go to the toilet and fast." Sophie bounded out of the car and into the gas station, not noticing the chaos or lack of shop attendant when she rushed inside.

"Does your stomach hurt?" Amirah asked Rachel, who had not recovered as fast as Sophie had. At least Sophie's body seemed to be purging the toxin. Rachel's body was not. Instead, the girl was in agony and starting to burn up.

"My head and stomach feel like they are on fire,"

Rachel mumbled, grabbing her stomach as wave after wave of pain hit.

Oh no, oh no, Amirah thought, watching helplessly while Rachel writhed in pain. She kept checking her phone; why had he not called her back. Amirah needed help for Rachel. She slid back into the driver's seat. Her hands shook as she sent a text to the only two people she trusted right now and hoped they would get back to her. She knew there was no way they could go to an ordinary hospital.

"Marvelous work in there, Dracula," Sophie, not looking too well, said as she climbed into the back seat next to Rachel. "Rachel," she whispered, nudging her to keep her awake. "Wake up," she said, wincing as another cramp hit her. "Seriously, what was in that antidote?" Sophie looked at Amirah questioningly as she still tried to get it off her tongue.

"It smelled like blood, but I don't think it belonged to humans or paranormal, or at least none I know of." Amirah shook her phone in frustration.

"Did you keep the vials?" Sophie asked before vomiting once again. Amirah nodded and pointed to the standing in the middle compartment.

Another grueling moan ripped through Rachel's lips as both Amirah and Sophie noted a new blood pool gathered around Rachel's waist, making Sophie hiss. "You need to go to a hospital now!"

"We can't go to a hospital; that is too risky!" Amirah panicked, then dialed the number she had recently sent an SOS text to.

~ ~ ~

He could hear voices through the darkness and pain.

"Rachel?" an angry male voice echoed around the room. "You were not authorized to go anywhere near those two girls," the man hissed.

Who was Rachel? He pried his heavy eyelids open; his tongue felt strange as he battled to find his voice to ask the man who Rachel was. He must have been able to get something out as he heard footsteps heading his way; he tried to lift his head, but it was too heavy.

"I thought you said he was heavily sedated?" a voice he thought he recognized said to him.

"He was," there was that weird voice he had heard in his dreams, the distorted one with the hideous face.

"I can vouch for that, sir," a female voice said, also vaguely familiar to him.

Why was he struggling to lift his head or talk? Had he had a stroke? Luka's mind was cloudy.

"His body seems to build up a resistance to the serum faster than anything we have seen. The more we give him, the faster he is building up a resistance."

"We need to move up the time frame," the angry man's voice was close now, but all he could see was the man's very expensive shoes. Everything went black as they once again injected him with what felt like fire. Just before the world went black, he heard a voice calling to him from far away.

Finding a Dragon

"SO, WHOSE CLINIC IS THIS AGAIN?" SOPHIE REALLY FELT like she looked and she was not happy about getting sick all over the outside of her new car. "Because I think I saw it once on Psycho Killers and Their Lairs." Sophie looked around the very, very, very old hospital that had probably been abandoned somewhere in the eighteen hundreds by the looks of the equipment she had just passed.

"It belongs to the only two people we can trust right now," Amirah was carrying Rachel.

They got to a door that looked like it was made from solid lead, like what a fallout shelter door looked like.

"Are we going into some sort of nuclear-type lock-down?" Sophie asked, knocking on the lead door.

"Stop that!" Amirah hissed. "You really should not touch every shiny thing you see." She watched as Sophie stepped back, taking a bite of yet another candy bar. "Nor should you eat so much sugar, especially after being poisoned."

"I'm hungry," Sophie said. "I threw up most of the little I ate today on my brand-new car door."

Amirah shook her head, and then told Sophie to be quiet for a minute as she made a weird tapping pattern on the door. They waited, the door flew open, and Sophie nearly choked on her candy bar as a Greek Adonis with brown eyes and blond hair smiled at them.

"Amirah," the blonde-haired greeted and immediately took Rachel from her. "Here, let me help you." He moved back, holding the door open. "Come in," and Amirah introduced him as they stepped through.

"This is Theo. Theo, that's Rachel in your arms and this, is Sophie." Amirah's brows creased as she noted the red flush and shy look, Sophie gave the man, and that is when she picked up the scent. On no, Amirah thought Sophie was an innocent. Just great; add another complication into the mix. She then glared at Theo, who had just noticed that too.

~ ❤ ~

"What else do you have in that bag of yours, Mary Poppins?" Theo asked Sophie. Amirah watched them closely, not happy with Theo's fascination with Sophie.

"Don't worry about him; I will keep an eye on them," Troy, Theo's twin, but with dark hair and blue eyes, told Amirah.

"I am just surprised that he is so interested in someone so young and not in his usual Lothario way," Amirah worried.

"So, do you think she is onto something?" Amirah asked Troy, bringing the conversation back to the poison and Sophie's theory about the dragon.

"I thought the Dream Catcher became extinct almost three thousand years ago?" Although, according to Sophie, there were whispers of a baby one. By baby, she meant it was still in its first century, so it could be anywhere from newborn to one-hundred.

"I do think she is onto something," Troy spun the samples in the centrifuge. "She is one scarily, smart young woman." Troy said, groaning as Sophie and his brother started discussing Star Wars yet again. "I think that is another reason the girl fascinates him. He has never met a human that could match his intellect, and I think that girl may even exceed it."

"I knew she was smart, but that is on another level," Amirah whistled while something else started to niggle at Amirah. "Can I have those blood samples you took from the girls again, please?"

~ ~ ~

"Are you sure this is the place?" Theo whispered to Sophie. The building looked like an abandoned warehouse.

"Yes," she whispered back. "Now hold the light steady." She clicked open the secure door to the facility, and they crept in.

"It's this way," Sophie followed the device on her wrist until they came to a door. She pushed it open, her eyes lit up as they fell on a cage. "Look there," she pointed to the glass cage.

Theo edged into the room and grabbed the cage making sure it was closed as the dragon started to hiss.

"Easy little fellow," Theo cooed, "This is a rescue

operation," he told the dragon and was surprised when it looked at him and relaxed.

"Now, let's get out of here," Theo walked to the door while Sophie rifled through the desks.

"Okay, give me a minute," Sophie said, scooping something off the desk and into her trusty satchel.

Theo and Sophie snuck down the passage towards the door. They had to duck into a room when a guard came out of a room talking on his phone and leaving the door slightly ajar. When he passed then and disappeared into another room, they quickly took off towards the exit, except something in the room the guard had come out of caught Sophie's eye.

Ignoring Theo's warning, she pushed her way into the room calling, "Luka."

Sophie ran towards Luka, accidentally tripping an alarm. The sound of guards descending upon them could be heard.

Theo opened out his arms like he was going in for a hug, but when he drew them back together, the six restrained, unconscious prisoners were brought closer. Sophie looked up at Theo, confused and amazed as he stood before them, large golden glowing wings protruding from his back.

The guards burst through the door in time to witness the prisoners, and the intruders disappear in a cloud of gold.

~ ~ ~

Sirens sounded in the secure joint PSI-HSA facility.

"How did this happen?" the general's anger resounded around the room.

"As far as we can tell, the girl managed to override the security," an officer informed the general.

"She is very good at doing things like that," the man in the grotesque mask piped in.

"If you had captured her when you were supposed to, we would still have our leverage and our dragon." The general glared at the man, "tell me again how they escaped."

"When we entered the room, a man with golden wings made out of light covered all the prisoners, and they vanished." the soldier swallowed, thinking he had just encountered an angel.

"Get the other three prisoners ready. We have some more videos to make for dear Amirah." The general looked at the men in the room with a sadistic smile. "It is time to up the stakes to force Amirah to get the final piece of the puzzle for the plan."

FOURTEEN

The Boys Are Back

LUKA'S WHOLE BODY WAS ON FIRE; HE FELT LIKE HE WAS literally going to burst into flames. He needed water, so he tried to sit up, only to find he could not move. His eyes flew open. He was restrained to what looked like a hospital bed. He swayed, his body trying to break free, but the restraints felt like a shock collar, as every time he yanked at them, he got zapped.

He turned his head, was that Rachel lying in that bed? He turned his head to the other side; he could see three separate beds. The one next to him was occupied by Josh. Both Rachel and Josh were not moving and, like him, had drips feeding into their arms. He needed to get them out of wherever the hell they were and find Amirah and Sophie because they were both in grave danger. He pulled against his restraints, but the tiny shocks seemed to paralyze his limbs for a few minutes each time they were activated.

An idea came to Luka; maybe he had a way to reach Amirah. She had told him about how vampires can track or mentally connect with a person by taking a sample of their blood. All it took was a few drops on their tongue to link the hunter and the prey. The link lasted up to seven days or until a new sample of blood was tasted. The scary part of that story was that every agent and employee at both the HSA and PSI had blood samples on file. Typically, the samples were held by the druids, but Luka and Josh had recently found out that even the Druids were no longer who they appeared to be. Now that this new group had control of the druids, they had the capabilities to find, manipulate, and control any creature they wanted on the planet. A drop or two of blood on the tongue linked vampire and prey for a few days, but injecting the prey's blood into the vampire linked the vampire to the prey's mind indefinitely.

He needed to concentrate; if she could find him, surely he could find her if they were linked? He let himself relax and think about her. He could see her as clear as day he reached out for her, calling her name. Luka could see her reaching for him, and he reached for her. Before their fingers could touch, pain sliced through his torso, and the darkness floated him away.

~ ~ ~

"Luka, I'm here," Amirah called to him. "Wake up, please," she leaned over and kissed his brow. They had woken up Josh and Quinton, but Luka had been given very high doses of sedatives to keep him knocked out while they were being held captive.

"Mm," a slow smile touched his lips. "I had the weirdest dream," he said with his eyes still closed, missing Amirah's eyes tearing up and a look of sheer relief on her face. He tried to reach out for her but found he was still restrained. His eyes opened. Was he still dreaming?

"Easy," Amirah said as she undid the restraints on his wrist. "You were fighting us like a demon and nearly knocked Sophie out." Luka's face went ashen as he tried to sit up but found his body was still restrained.

"She is okay, just spitting mad at you, though," Amirah laughed as he lay back, relieved.

Amirah went willingly when Luka pulled her down next to him on the bed, saying, "You were telling me about your weird dream," she laid her head on his chest and closed her eyes. He had given them such a scare.

Luka gave a soft laugh, smoothing her hair, as he continued, "There were these crazy vampires, one of which broke into my apartment and turned my life upside down," he planted kisses on her head, pulling her up, hungry for a taste of her lips; he ignored the slicing pain in his gut.

"Seriously, I am going to need so much therapy when this is over," Rachel threw a pillow at them. "Do you mind? There are others in this room."

Amirah laughed, rolling off the bed as a barrage of pillows hit them from all sides of the room. Before Luka could respond to the pillow bombs, he grabbed his stomach in pain just before vomiting up a pool of blood, and once again passing out.

"Luka!" Amirah screamed, her head instantly going to his chest. His heart was still beating, but the blood he had brought up was starting to smell rancid.

"Troy, Theo, Soph, get in here now!" Josh shouted down the passage.

"What are you all doing out of ..." Sophie's eyes dropped to the pool of blood around Luka. The look in

Amirah's pleading eyes told Sophie that Luka did not have long. That meant that soon Luka, Josh, and Quinton were going to end up like the other two PSI agents they had rescued.

～～～

Sophie turned and marched out of the room, storming towards the lab, where she grabbed four syringes.

"You cannot do this, Soph," Theo pleaded with her as he followed her into the lab. "You know the consequences of giving your blood to anyone else, especially a vampire."

"Well, they are dying anyway, so what difference will it make? If this does not work, there won't be any mind links because they will all be dead." She grabbed a band for a tourniquet.

The dragon hissed and started pacing in its new luxury cage Sophie had made for it, complete with a little forest and heat lamps to mimic the warm sun. Theo could not explain it at first, but Sophie and the dragon had formed an instant connection. They could even communicate telepathically, and she had named the dragon Dreamy, which would be apt for a Dream Catcher dragon; however, when these creatures were provoked, there was nothing dreamy about them. Their venom literally boiled a person from the inside out and turned them to ash if injected into flesh. At the same time, the dragon's mist would paralyze its prey and completely numb it.

"Even Dreamy agrees with me that this is a terrible idea," Theo tried to stop her from leaving the room.

"Please, Theo, I have to do this," Sophie's eyes were

glazed with unshed tears. "My brother sacrificed every-thing to save myself and my sister from our father." She swallowed. "He even got killed, stopping us from being taken to our Godfather, who apparently was even worse than my dad." She put her hand on his chest. "My brother wanted Luka to find me, as he knew that Luka would keep me safe. Now it is my turn to help Luka, Rachel, and the others fighting to stop this sick faction."

Theo knew he was in so much trouble with young women who had stolen his heart. When his kind finally gave their heart, they did so for eternity, so he did some-thing that he knew was wrong, but she had given him no choice.

"Then take this," a beautiful golden feather appeared in his hand. "Tell me you accept it so that it will keep you safe," he knew that what he was doing was not ethical, but he knew no other way to protect her.

"It is beautiful," Sophie took the feather. "Of course, I will accept it," she said innocently. Then, she thanked him with a thank you kiss, before moving around him and barreling out the door, not realizing the implications of her innocent actions.

Dreamy hissed and swished his tail, the dragon's strange green and yellow eyes boring into him.

"Don't judge me," Theo told the dragon. "I didn't see you doing anything to help."

"You lost the dragon, both girls, and the hostages."

Gold robes swished as the man swirled around to glare at the three people kneeling in front of him. "Oh, get up!" he said impatiently, his bejeweled fingers gesturing his impatience. Centuries of work and careful planning were almost undone by their incompetence.

"We will go with your plan," the gilded robed man pointed to the general. "But make no mistake; this is your last chance. Do not let me down again and get me my property back. ALL OF IT!" With that, he left in a flurry of golden robes.

Jeweled fingers caressed the weird-looking contraption that joined two chairs that looked a lot like dentist chairs. One faced forward, the other backward, while two laser helmets were hooked overhead. This was his creation, legacy, and way of restoring his species back to their glory. No, he thought, their species would be more glorious than ever before. This time, no magic would be able to leave his species barren and having to continue their line like they were some sort of disease.

This chair enabled him to milk the power of any magical creature. However, he had to admit he still loved the thrill of torturing and bending creatures to his will. He loved the smell of their fear and the taste of complete surrender before having them beg to let him take their essence.

He ran his hand over the special compartment in the middle of the machine and smiled. There was one who had dared to defy him. One turned his people against him, one that still plagued his empire and instilled rebellion. Anger boiled inside him and cooled only as he plotted his revenge and dreamt of savoring that person's suffering. He no longer needed permission to get what he wanted; he could simply take it.

FIFTEEN

The Antidote

"So, explain it to me in plain English, how exactly Dreamy's venom works?" Luka asked Sophie, wishing she would take the creature off his bed. Right now, the two-foot dragon was lying on its back with its feet up in the air while Sophie tickled its soft belly. After the hell he had just been through, he did not want to be anywhere near him or her for that matter.

"When he wants to eat a small creature like a rat or a cat," Sophie showed Luka the small holes near the miniature dragon's nose, "he will first paralyze it with a mist that sprays out of these openings. I call them his vents."

"How far can he spray?" Luka asked her, trying to visualize how a gas could be made from it.

"Well, not sure to a precise degree but around ten to twelve feet." She scratched the dragon on the soft skin beneath his neck, and the dragon kicked his legs like a dog would when tickled on a ticklish spot. "Aww, you are such a cutie."

"That is quite far for his size, though, isn't it?" Luka

asked Sophie, and then was shocked by what Sophie told him next.

"Yes, but he is not going to stay this small forever," Sophie told him, laughing as the dragon flopped over and then nuzzled Sophie like a cat did when they wanted attention.

"Excuse me?" Luka asked his face going white. "You mean to tell me that Dreamy is still going to grow?"

"Yup, to at least another forty to forty-five feet as he is a male," Sophie shrugged, then lifted her new friend up and showed Luka his tail, which was currently encased in a silver sleeve Sophie had Troy fashion for it.

"They do not have very sharp teeth, so they will slice the prey with either their very poisonous claws or razor-sharp tail. Their tail has millions of tiny hollow spikes on it." She applied pressure on one of Dreamy's paws, and out popped really vicious talons. "This is where their venom gets injected through, like a snake's hollow fangs. The dragon's talons are also hollow, and when they extract them, they immediately fill with poison."

Luka looked at her worriedly as she handled the dragon with absolutely no fear.

"Shouldn't his fingers and toes have some sort of restraints like his tail does?" Luka asked, leaning away from the creature.

"Nah, he won't hurt anyone," she put Dreamy back down on Luka's bed. "Well, at least, no one here anyway."

"They can only eat food that is very charred or has turned to ash." Sophie continued to tell Luka, "The mist not only paralyzes but anesthetizes the prey. I don't actually think they feel anything when the venom burns their prey from the inside." Sophie was so involved with telling Luka about her findings that she did not notice the look of fear on his face. "If a bit of the venom drops onto the skin, it will eat into the flesh like acid."

"So the factions found a way to weaponizing Dreamy's venom and his mist?" Luka felt quite sick at the thought of what harm could be done with that sort of weapon. "Your blood has built up antibodies against the venom from the antidote you took?" Luka asked, trying to clarify how her blood was able to cure all four of them.

"Well …" Sophie picked up Dreamy to keep him as a barrier between them, "My body somehow naturally warded off the toxin itself."

Luka stared at her in disbelief, "I don't understand."

"Basically, I think I am the antidote," Sophie told him, and then ran out the room with her dragon before Luka had time to say anything else.

SIXTEEN

The Plot Thickens

LUKA STOOD STARING AT THE DRAGON LOUNGING beneath its sun lamp. If he was in any other line of work, he might just be freaking out by now with everything that had been going on around him this past week. He never thought he would be on the run. Wanted by his own agency, with fugitive vampires, two human women he was rather angry with, and whatever Amirah's brothers were. Yeah, that had really shocked him finding out Amirah had biological brothers, one of whom had magical wings.

He looked at the black cup of coffee he held in hands, wishing it was something a lot stronger. He turned around and felt like a school teacher about to give the entire class detention by the way eight pairs of eyes were looking at him.

"So, let me get this straight," he pointed at Alison and Rachel. "You two are sisters?" The two young women nodded; Alison was munching on the hamburger and fries she had commandeered from Luka after consuming hers.

"Yes, our father was a horrible man. He had a bad temper and would take it out on my mom and then Bradley, our older brother." Rachel told him, "My mother met Amirah at one of Marog's women empowerment seminars."

"Lynn and I became good friends, and I gave her a job as my assistant." Amirah continued Rachel's story. "She told me about her problems with her husband, and I was trying to help her and her children escape the man." Amirah told them all, "I never got to meet Lynn's children as the night we were going to move them was the night Lynn's husband pushed her down the stairs and killed her." Amirah still got angry and sad when she thought of her dear friend and all she had to suffer.

"It was that night during all the commotion that our brother got us out of the house, and we ran away." Rachel continued, "My mom had told Brad to find Amirah. Only Brad got caught by our Godfather while he was waiting for Amirah and was beaten to an inch of his life."

"That is the day you found me," Sophie told Luka while she eyed Quinton's almost untouched hamburger.

"The day you pickpocketed me, you mean?" Luka told her, and she grinned before she started to steal Quinton's chips.

"I went to find Brad, and when I got back, Soph was gone," Rachel continued the story. "Amirah had found Brad nearly dead, but she helped him the only way she could, or he would have died," Rachel said softly. "Then she came to find me and in the nick of time too." Rachel smiled at Amirah, the fondness the girl had for Amirah shining in her eyes. "I told Amirah that Soph was safe as she had come back and tried to get me to go to Luka. But I knew that if we kept our distance, our father would have a harder time tracking us down."

"You could have told me, Soph," Luka said softly. "But I understand why you didn't." He smiled at the young woman he had been looking after since the day they had met.

"They didn't tell me either," Amirah assured Luka she was not in on this. "I only knew that Rachel's sister was safe and it was better if I did not know where she was."

"What happened to Brad?" Luka asked.

"We were hoping you could answer that," Amirah said. "He was part of your unit, but you would have known him as Bry."

"Bry," Luka now knew for certain how Amirah had healed Bradley. Bry was one of the clan vampires assigned to his elite team by the HSA.

"A few days before Brad was deployed to go on your last mission, he gave me a drive and said that if anything happened to him, I had to get this to you." Rachel gave Luka a tiny drive.

Luka looked at Sophie, brows raised, "Do you know what is on here?"

"Nope." Sophie was sharing Quinton's burger with Dreamy.

"Soph!" Luka gave her a look that she knew meant he knew her better than that.

"Okay, yes, I do," Sophie rolled her eyes. "My father was a scientist. He worked for the government doing genetic experiments." She had plugged the drive in and projected the contents on the file to the large screen that hung on the wall.

All eyes moved to the screen and then immediately

back to Soph in shocked surprise. "Surprise," she gave them an emoji type toothy smile. "My siblings and I are his first successful genetic experiment."

Theo and Troy moved towards the screen, dumbfounded by the data there.

Troy turned back to her, saying, "That is why that mad vampire stalker was probably after you."

"Well, now that I know this, you are probably right," Sophie shrugged, and then pulled up another piece of information that had them all go quiet. "The doctor that Amirah is accused of beating to death was operating under a false name."

Rachel gasped as they pulled the picture up on the screen. "That's our father," she rasped.

"And the person beating him up is not Amirah but one of the PSI agents we rescued with Luka, Josh, Quinton, and Nicholas." All heads turned to the vampire they had rescued as well. "By the look on Luka's face, he is lucky he is now a pile of ash in the lab."

"Nicholas, according to you," Luka eyed the vampire suspiciously, he was once of the purebreds, "you were drained of any abilities you may have had in some weird contraption that looked like you were at the dentist," Luka asked, not looking convinced. He knew who Nicholas was and what he could do.

"Okay, so we know that the faction wants Sophie, Rachel, Nicholas, and probably their dragon back," Luka ran his fingers through his hair as he paced back and forth. "They are out for mine and Amirah's blood because we have Fuller's daughters and a drive full of information on their experiment." He ran his hands through his hair even more as he paced again.

"They cannot be happy about the way Amirah's politics inspires woman to rise up as we know they are a faction that believes the male sex are akin to Gods. Most of the movements that have arisen have been inspired by groups Amirah has either started or supported."

"No, I am not responsible for every movement that arises because they are sick of being bullied," Amirah denied her role in that, and she tried very hard to keep herself out of politics of any kind. She learned a long time ago how ruthless politicians could be.

"Probably also because she basically cut off the head of the last Rites of Adam faction in the eighteen hundreds," Theo injected, getting a glare from his brother and sister.

"What?" Luka asked, clearly agitated at all the information being kept from him.

"It was nothing," Amirah punched Theo on the arms, saying under her breath. "I am sure that this faction is some copycat faction of that one."

"Don't you think it is just a bit too much of a coincidence that this faction is coming after you, full steam ahead?" Luka asked her, fear for her and frustration at their current situation, bringing him to a boiling point. "Don't you see? The faction now has control over two agencies that keep the peace between the supernatural world and the human world."

Amirah eyed Luka, and she knew full well what that meant and did not need him trying to put her in the middle of it all. "I still do not see why you would think this is about me?" Amirah glared at Luka.

Luka did not want to fight with her, but he also knew she was not being honest with him, or rather, everyone in the room. He saw she was angry and knew her well enough to know she was not going to say any more on the subject now. So, he turned back to Rachel; there were still a few things he needed the sisters to clear up for him.

"What happened to Bry, sorry, Bradley?" He asked Rachel as he knew Sophie had spoken about her sister to him but not her brother.

"Bradley started the Bronlynn movement," Rachel said quietly. "Bron was my mother's maiden name." Rachel looked at Quinton; now that she knew who he was, she thought it was time he knew. "Bradley was killed defending his new wife-to-be, Jackie Banks, in the raid on Bronlynn's coven." A tear rolled down her cheek as Quinton hugged her, sharing her pain.

"That is why you were so infuriated with me when I came to the office to see Amirah," Luka said to her. Her hate and hostility towards him had been a bit odd. She nodded her in affirmation. "You thought I had killed your brother."

"Sophie did not believe you would have done what the files said you had. So, she continued to dig. Around seven months ago, she found out that the raid had been done by another off-the-books team," Rachel told him.

"But my sister was not talking to me or taking my calls. She had not taken them since she found out about the raid and refused to believe Luka was responsible."

Sophie took over Rachel's story, "Someone had told Rachel that Luka's team had wiped out the coven and that he was dangerous." Sophie took a deep breath as she recalled that it was around the same time her stalker showed up.

"I got the general to assign Amirah to Luka, so I had

a way of getting back into my sister's life. But also because I found information about Amirah suddenly being redacted and information about Luka's mission being changed," Sophie told the surprised people in the room. "I also found out about some weird cross-species off-book project that involved some sort of host or something." Sophie once again moved something from her laptop to the screen, "It was in a language I have never seen, and I am still trying to decipher."

Troy and Theo looked at each other strangely; they knew that language and read what was written there.

Theo turned to Rachel, "I am sorry, this is probably so insensitive of me, but who is the seed of your offspring?"

Rachel looked at Theo, confused for a moment before what he asked sank in, "Oh, you mean, who is the father of my child?"

All eyes spun to Rachel, "By your looks, I take it none of you knew Rachel was pregnant?" Luka asked them.

"You did?" Amirah, still annoyed at him, was surprised.

"Yes, I felt the second heartbeat when I lifted her up in your office to move her aside."

"It's not hers," Sophie said. "She is a surrogate for a couple." All eyes were back on Sophie questioningly; once again, she shrugged, "So, I kept track of my sister."

"Soph is right," Rachel said. "A nice man and his partner wanted to have a child. I had met them about two months before at the coffee shop near Amirah's apartment." Rachel told them. "They told me about the adoption process and how they had been waiting for either that or a surrogate." Rachel touched her stomach that was only slightly swollen. "So, I volunteered to be their surrogate as it also paid really well, which meant I could get my sister away from Luka and pay for her college."

"Rachel!" Amirah said. "You could have come to me. You know I would have helped." Amirah walked over to Rachel and touched her stomach. Something was not quite right, the child's heartbeat was all wrong. Her eyes flew up and met Sophie's. Something in Sophie's expression said she knew as she shook her head, warning Amirah not to say anything.

⌣ ⌣ ⌣

"Do you still think this is not about you or your politics?" Luka asked Amirah as they exited the clinic.

Amirah looked at her phone as it was almost time for the synthesized voice to call. Their latest video had been another direct attack on Amirah. The faction wanted her to know that this was not over, and they still had leverage over her. They held the last two of her clan members, Matthew and Bart, along with a hostage, but they could not see who it was.

"I think there is something wrong with Rachel's baby," Amirah said, taking him by surprise and steering the subject away from the current one.

"Is this your way of changing the subject?" Luka looked at her infuriated that she still refused to believe this was somehow centered around her.

"No," Amirah was now getting infuriated with him. He was like one of those dogs that when they bit down on something, their jaws locked. "I think her baby is a vampire."

"That is not possible," Luka said. "Nowhere is it documented that vampires can breed. I thought cross-species procreation between human and magical creatures, especially vampires, was impossible." He shook his head, "I mean, can vampires even breed?"

"How do you think the first vampires came about?" Amirah asked him a bit astounded at his words. "The stork?"

"No, of course not," Luka said, seeing he had offended her. He had not meant to do that.

"We are a species, not a disease, Luka," Amirah's cheeks flamed. "Well, at least, we used to be able to breed." Her voice dropped.

"I'm sorry, Amirah," Luka walked up to her, cupping her arms with his hand as he looked down at her, saying, "I truly did not mean to insult you. In all the information we have on your species, nothing is documented about breeding. We only know that your fangs contain a substance that can induce a feeling of euphoria, can heal, and, if given in high enough doses, can change a being's ..." Both their eyes widened. "They have been experimenting with not a vampire and human DNA, but all kinds of creatures."

"Both the girls' DNA has been altered," Amirah told Luka. "The reason Rachel did not recover as quickly as Sophie must have been because of the baby."

"Yet they are both still human, according to Troy," Luka continued. "But there were markers in their blood that showed they carried the same antidote in their blood as Dreamy."

"Yes, no dragon can poison another dragon with its

own type of venom," Amirah agreed and added what she knew about dragons. "I think the girls were born to an already genetically modified mother. Their mother was the one they were genetically modifying."

When Amirah's phone rang, she hit the answer button.

"Hello Amirah," the ugly synthesized voice came on the line. "Is that Luka I hear in the background?"

"What do you want?" Amirah asked the man, thing, or whatever it was.

"Well, at first, we just wanted the necklace and the girls back," the terrible voice told her, "but now you have stolen a lot more from us. The thing is, Amirah, we gave you a chance with the girls. But now you have to pay the price for stealing from us." The voice sneered. "But even though you stole from us, we are still going to be fair and let you choose which of your beloved elder clan vampires dies," the voice laughed. "Oh, and you are not allowed to choose the mystery guest as he is not leverage for you."

"No, don't harm any of them. Just tell me what you want," Amirah panicked now that she knew they had Bart and Matthew. The last two of her clan who had not answered their message or phones.

"Tick tock, Amirah. You have one minute to decide, or I will decide for you," the voice warned her.

"I am going to hunt you down and …"

"Tut tut. Time is up," the voice tormented her. "Let's see which one, which one. Ah, I know the one I like the least." There was a swishing noise, her phone binged, her hand started to shake as she watched the video of Bart being beheaded with his own sword. She dropped the phone and fell to her knees, sobbing. It was all just too much.

Luka picked up the phone, his gut burning with rage he hissed into the phone. "We will find you." He warned but was cut off by another voice that was vaguely familiar to him.

"Make sure Amirah delivers the necklace, the girls, Josh, Quinton, the phoenix, the hunter, and our dragon."

Luka noted a catch in the new voice as it said one of the names.

"She has until the mixer on Saturday night, which is where she will bring everything we have asked for. If she does not, not only will she be responsible for the death of her oldest clan vampire, but also for over a hundred innocents tending the mixer." With that, the line went dead.

Luka knelt down next to Amirah and pulled her into his arms. Their eyes met, and his heart stopped when he saw the agony in them. He knew those demons all too well. Her eyes searched him as if looking for some form of salvation, but all he could do was comfort her.

"It is not your fault," he told her softly, his large hands cupping her beautiful face. "We will find that monster, and he will pay," Luka promised her.

They were so close together their foreheads were almost touching. They could feel the heat from each other's bodies. A need like nothing either of them had experienced before except when they were together rose up inside them.

"I love you, Amirah," Luka whispered as their lips meshed together.

Amirah pulled back and looked into Luka's eyes.

Dark with desire and filled with love, saying, "I love you too, Luka, more than I ever thought it possible to love another being."

Their hungry lips found each other again as the world faded around them. They fed their frenzied desire, cradled by the grass of the field that ran around the abandoned hospital.

SEVENTEEN

The Truth About Amirah

"IT SEEMS THE FACTION IS AFTER A NECKLACE CALLED the Stone of Zara," Amirah told the group gathered in the area of the clinic that had become the living room.

"The essence of the Princess Supreme and the key to the Seat of Power?" Sophie asked in surprise. If the legends were correct about the necklace, it unlocked the Seat of Power. The source of all magic and freed the most ruthless vampire from his eternal prison.

"Yes, but how did you know about that?" Amirah asked her while she watched Sophie fidget in her satchel and pull out an ancient journal that almost made Amirah's heart stop in fear. "Where did you get that?" Amirah's voice held a touch of panic.

"I got it along with a whole lot of ancient texts when we got Dreamy," Sophie informed her. "Theo is teaching me to read the ancient vampire language." She told Amirah proudly, missing the look on Amirah's face as she glared at her younger brother.

"I believe it is a book of shadows type book and

journal of the Princess Supreme." Sophie continued excitedly, oblivious to Amirah's growing discomfort at the mention of the book.

"The necklace is no myth, fairy tale, or legend," Amirah informed them, aware that everyone in this room, except for Rachel, had heard about the necklace and the Seat of Power. "Neither is the Seat of Power," her voice dropped, and she looked at Troy for support.

"If the faction gets their hands on the necklace, they not only have the key to unlock it; they also have the main part of the map to get to it," Troy continued the story for Amirah.

"How many other parts of the map are there and where are they?" Luka asked, his gut instinct was kicking into overdrive once again, and he had a feeling he knew those pieces were close by.

"Part of it is magically tattooed on me," Theo told them as he stood up and lifted up his shirt to reveal his back. It was severely scarred with what looked like brutal lash marks. Theo breathed in, and as he breathed out, he allowed them to see part of the map that appeared like someone was drawing it on his back in front of their eyes.

"I have one as well," Troy told them but did not show his back. "And so does Amirah."

"Only Rohan knows where the necklace is and the other two parts of the map," Theo pulled his shirt back down.

"Theo, your back…" Sophie's eyes were filled with sorrow for the pain those lashings must have caused.

"There have been many times through the ages people have wanted our birthright," Theo said softly, smiling down at her.

"I can tell you where the other two pieces of the map are." Nicholas breathed out and stepped into the spotlight. "They were entrusted to myself and twin brother Vincent who the faction still holds captive."

"Well, that is just great then," Josh whistled. "Here in this room is just about everything the faction needs to unleash hell."

"Where is the necklace?" Luka asked Amirah, Theo, and Troy. The three exchanged a weird look before saying together, "With our cousin Rohan McGarth." Luka, Josh, and Quinton stood gaping at them as what they just said sunk in.

"Rohan is Ronald McGarth's grandson. From his son that was killed by the high priestess Odette," Sophie recalled the story from the journal. "Odette killed all of Ronald's family except his eldest daughter, who ran away with her oldest son ..." Sophie's eyes grew huge as she turned to Amirah and her two siblings.

"Yes, Soph, we are Ronald McGarth's heirs to his throne and grandchildren of two of the most powerful beings on the planet," Troy confirmed what he knew the girl had just figured out.

"You are Zara, the Supreme Princess, and next in line for both the Silver Valley and the Okapi Grove."

"Amirah is the power source for the Stone of Zara and the only one who can unlock both the magical silver mines and the Okapi Grove."

"If that happens, the world will fall back into very dark times," Amirah ended the story softly.

The team was not ready to know what would be unleashed on the world should those two sources be unlocked. Amirah looked at everyone gathered around her, and she hoped they would never have to find out.

"So, it looks like we have a high-profile vampire to go visit?" Luka put together the next part of their plan because getting to Rohan was not going to be easy. He was a vampire that had a lot of eyes watching him.

EIGHTEEN

Keeper of the Stone of Zara

THE ONLY ONE WHO COULD RETRIEVE THE STONE OF Zara was Rohan. He was a high-profile ancient vampire and was one of the most powerful ones still alive. As a result, he was also monitored around the clock by both the HSA and PSI.

Amirah and the team had to use secret tunnels that ran beneath the city to go see him. Rohan was a tall, well-dressed vampire, the likes none of them had seen before. Both of his parents died when he was young, so Rohan had grown up under the strict rule of Ronald. Not able to take his tyranny any longer or being subjected to endless abuse, Rohan was the one who orchestrated Ronald's capture and entrapment at the Okapi Grove.

As the Okapi Grove sat upon the sacred land of the lost coven, it was well protected by the tribal elders. Only Rohan could walk upon the holy ground and transcend worlds to where Ronald was now trapped.

"I am surprised to see you and your hunter here," Rohan addressed Amirah.

"Why is that cousin?" Amirah asked him, refusing his offer of refreshment and stopping Sophie from doing the same.

"All of you have huge bounties on your heads," Rohan smiled down at Amirah before his amber eyes took in the merry band of teammates. "In fact, you have dug yourself so far into a trench this time that if I were you, I would probably go to the Okapi Grove and lay low there for a while." Rohan laughed. "I hear Ronald has quite the vineyard this year made from the souls of the damned." He winked at Rachel's, seeing her shocked look.

"What do you know about the situation?" Amirah asked him because if anyone would know what was going on, he would. Rohan was also the most well-connected vampire that all had his ear to the ground.

"It seems an old colleague of Ronald's has found a way to work around the curse of Odette," Rohan told them, which made Amirah balk. "That is all I know other than I have been told that I too may have my own problems from that faction."

"I need the Stone of Zara," Amirah told him. Rohan looked at her, surprised for a minute, then put down his drink and cocked his head at her before saying, "Really?"

"Well. Not really, but I need it." The two exchanged a look.

Rohan nodded before saying, "I will get you what you want." He turned and left the room without another word.

NINETEEN

The Mixer

Quinton and Josh all but pulled Sophie towards the large ballroom door, stopping when they heard a warning hiss. Both pairs of eyes looked at her clutch and then back at her questionably.

"Please tell me you did not get Dreamy to shrink down into your purse again before we left?" Josh asked, glaring at Quinton, who was supposed to check her purse. "You know he needs to be in the cage."

"What makes you think I have Dreamy in there?" Sophie asked and then stepped into the ballroom to distract them.

"Soph, where did you get that golden feather?" Quinton whispered; she had promised to tell him later if he promised not to tell on her about Dreamy.

Before she could reply, they were joined by the rest of the crew. All eyes fell on the large silver framed ruby Amirah had around her neck. A feeling of unease surrounded them all with the necklace being exposed like another piece of jewelry.

"I thought you could not wear silver," Sophie said to Amirah.

"The necklace's frame and chain were forged before the silver was poisoned," Amirah told her.

"The six targets are here," the man said over his earpiece as he watched Amirah, Luka, Sophie, Nicholas, Josh, and Quinton walk into the ballroom.

"Good," the general said.

"Amirah, there you are," Kayla Ambrose walked over to where the six of them stood. "I am so glad you came." She pouted prettily, her eyes moving past Amirah to Luka. "Luka? Is that you?" She looked at him, seductively before giving him a hug. Luka stiffened as she gave a soft laugh, her eyes meeting Quinton's.

"Quinton," Kayla said, completely ignoring Josh. Something about the way she said it captured Luka's attention.

"You know Quinton?" Amirah asked Kayla.

"Yes, unfortunately," Kayla said in clipped tones. "He is my ex-fiancé that dumped me because he is not a real man." She sneered, a flash of venom flickered in her eyes as she looked at Josh. But her tone belied her anger as she quickly gathered herself, linking her arm through Amirah's and commenting. "I love your necklace."

She steered them all towards the VIP booth, which

was a sizeable soundproof glass dome that looked down onto the ballroom. "I booked the entire dome," Kayla told them, inviting them all in. They followed her, keeping an eye out for the Rites of Adam members.

TWENTY

The Betrayal

"Amirah," a voice called, "is that you?"

"Johnny?" Amirah frowned as he walked into the booth. "What are you doing here?"

"I invited him." Kayla stepped up behind him.

"Amirah, meet my new girlfriend, Kayla Ambrose," Johnny told her rather smugly. "She is everything a man should have in a woman." He said, and laughed.

His laugh brought back fuzzy memories to Luka. He was about to lunge forward and grab the man when Sophie walked in with a plate full of food and froze, saying, "YOU!"

"Ah, so you do remember me still," Johnny turned around, looking pleased by the look on Sophie's face.

"Johnny, what is going ..." Before Amirah could complete her sentence, Luka had the vampire by the throat.

"I would put him down if I were you, soldier," Luka and Quinton spun as the sound of General Trent's voice.

"Grant?" Amirah said questioningly. "What are both of you doing here?"

"Hello Amirah," Grant looked at her with ice in his eyes.

"You know General Trent and Sophie's stalker?" Luka and Sophie looked at her with hurt expressions, clearly thinking she had betrayed them all.

"No," Amirah told them both. "That is Johnny and Grant, two of my clan vampires." Amirah looked at Josh, Quinton, and Nicholas. They also looked at her with the same betrayed expression.

"Kayla is a client of my dating service." Anger suddenly spurted up inside of her. She was tired of playing these stupid games; someone was going to give her answers.

"What is going on here, Grant?" Amirah asked him angrily. "Is this still about your project I refused to take part in or back?" Amirah could not believe that this may just all be about some silly revenge ploy.

"Oh, Amirah, this is only partly about you for a change," Grant sneered. Luka went to make a move, but Grant warned, "I will not hesitate to pull this trigger and then snack on her pureblood." Grant had put his arm around Sophie's neck and a gun to her side while he made a point of sniffing Sophie's tender young neck.

Amirah held Luka back; she still could not believe she had been betrayed by two of her own, and Kayla. Her mind was reeling; they had killed off their own clan members in horrific ways and lied to her.

"Find the others," Kayla ordered some of the soldiers that had surrounded them.

"Yes, General," the soldiers saluted Kayla and left. Luka and Quinton both looked at Kayla in surprise. She was the general that had tortured them in captivity both during that fateful mission and recently. Grant, who had been parading as General Trent for the past three years, was the one that authorized that mission. Johnny was the psycho who had stalked, terrorized, and tried to kidnap Sophie. It was slowly starting to make a bit of sense now.

"We are going to find the rest of our items anyway, or just resort to ugly means to find them," Grant said matter of factly. "So, why don't you save us the effort and tell us where Rachel and our dragon are?" Grant asked them.

"What do you want with Rachel?" Sophie asked Grant. Luka noticed Sophie's diversion tactic and her hand slipping into her purse. She really did bring that dragon! Luka thought, and then smiled to himself, thinking they should let Grant take Sophie. He would return her after she ate him out of house and home, questioned everything, and turned his kitchen into a science experiment.

"Well, child," Grant looked at her, beaming with pride, "your father and I engineered you and your sister." He looked her over and sighed. "Look at you, the perfect specimen of genetic enhancement." He shook his head as he said, "It was a pity we had to take down your brother." Grant smiled at the shock on her face, "He was the first vampire to be born to a human."

Sophie's eyes shot to Amirah.

"Bry begged me not to tell you or Rachel," Amirah told Sophie. Amirah had known there was something different about Bry, but she thought that Bry had been turned by another vampire. "I also thought he had been turned. I did not know he was born."

"Oh, yes, and he was magnificent," Grant looked Sophie over. "Your mother was fed various hormones to enhance her genetics." Grant laughed at what he told her next. "The stupid bitch actually thought she was taking hormones to help her conceive."

Sophie stiffened, "Don't talk about my mother like that." She hissed as anger boiled inside of her.

"You, your brother, and your sister are remarkable." Grant told her, and then cocked his head towards the ballroom. "But we will soon have a few hundred more like you." He told her. "Especially now, we know how well the female human body can carry a vampire."

He laughed at her look of disgust. "You are just like Amirah, aren't you?" His gaze was one of loathing, "Thinking women have some power because you can give birth. Yet I was the one who created you."

The little dragon snuck around the back of Sophie, clingy to her dress. "You are a bit deranged and archaic," Sophie told him for which she received a slap across the face from Grant, shocking the entire room as the sound resonated.

Johnny and Kayla laughed in sick delight, and at that moment soon shut up as Dreamy pushed himself away from Sophie and morphed into his full size.

Grant's eyes widened in shock as the dragon flew towards him but stopped when Sophie shouted, "No, Dreamy, get the others."

Grant's head turned around towards her, and Sophie punched him flying. Then Dreamy zapped him with his mist after zapping Kayla and Johnny.

"You and your women's empowerment movement," Grant's turned back to her, his eyes held nothing but hate. "Women are not supposed to question the stronger sex of the species." He battled to move his body as the paralytic slowly consumed him.

Josh walked up to him and punched Grant, knocking him out. "Does that stuff not paralyze their vocal cords?" he asked Sophie, who laughed, making Dreamy shrink down and climb back into her purse.

"Let's go find Rachel and get all those people out of here. I have a feeling this is not over," Luka took over command as they lifted Grant, Kayla, and Johnny onto chairs and tied them up with cable ties Sophie had in her purse. No one asked why she had them in her purse, though.

As they were about to head out of the door, both Luka and Amirah stopped. Luka could feel the evil ripple through the air as he had on that last mission and before entering Josh's house.

Amirah could smell him as his particular brand of sadistic pleasure permeated the air, sending those all too familiar chills of icy fear up her spine. At first, she felt paralyzed by the fear, but she was no longer a frightened young girl. She had faced evil more than once in her long life and overcame it; she was not going to bow down to it now.

As she turned to face the man that had tortured her and her brothers for almost a century, his voice made her skin crawl as he asked, "Going somewhere?"

TWENTY-ONE

The Showdown

THEY ALL TURNED AROUND TO FIND A MAN DRESSED IN gold robes, jewels adorning his fingers, and eyes that showed him to be one of the pure-bred ancient vampires. He was surrounded by the Rite of Adam soldiers, three of which held Rachel, Troy, and Theo.

"Darius," Amirah rasped, her eyes growing in fear when three soldiers came into the room with her brothers and Rachel in tow.

"It's the Pope guy that had Jeff shot," Sophie whispered to Luka as he pushed her behind him.

"Take those three fools away," Darius ordered his soldiers, pointing to the three tied up. "Deal with them as you did the rest." He calmly ordered Johnny's, Kayla's, and Grant's execution.

He indicated by crooking his finger for Rachel to follow him. Seeing she was under thrall, the soldier released her. While Amirah could see Rachel was trying to fight the thrall, she also knew the burning pain it caused when you tried to resist it. She shook her head at Rachel, indicating for the girl to go with it.

Darius hummed as he glided towards the group of them. They all started feeling like their bodies had melted into the floor and could not move.

"Don't try to fight it," Nicholas warned them. "It will make it worse and cause excruciating pain."

"He is right," Amirah whispered to them all.

"Where is Vincent, you sick bastard?" Nicholas spat at the gilded man, "What have you done to him?"

"Well, Nicholas, as you rudely escaped before offering me your essence, I decided to taste your brothers." Darius lifted his shoulder, making a face like he had just tasted a gourmet meal. "And I must say, this power is a lovely fit for me." He laughed as he watched the pain burn through Nicholas, who was trying to free himself to kill Darius. "Seriously, Nicholas, even if you were free, you know you don't have the guts to kill me." He sneered at Nicholas, looking at him with disappointment and disgust. "Honestly, it nearly pained me to have to use your brother instead."

He had moved in front of Amirah. His heavily jeweled fingers lifted the heavy blood ruby around her neck. "Ah, the Stone of Zara," he whispered, leaning in close to Amirah's face. He heard Luka's drawn breath and glanced up at Luka. Darius loved the man's discomfort and pain he was in trying to save Amirah.

"What do you want with us, Darius?" Amirah asked.

"Why, to undo what your paternal grandmother did to our kind," Darius told her.

"You and Ronald did that, not her," Amirah spat at him. "You and Ronald with your sick twisted thirst for power and ultimate male domination."

"Ah, little Zara," Darius ran his hand down Amirah's cheek. "Do you not remember the pleasure of our union?" His eyes turned towards Luka, seeing the fire and now rage burning there. "Did you not tell your hunter about the many nights you and I spent together?" He laughed as he watched Luka struggle to get out of the grips of Darius's thrall.

"You mean, the many nights you beat me and forced me to your will while you tortured my brothers?" Amirah spat back at him, keeping his eyes trained on her as she bit back the pain and moved her fingers towards Sophie's bag. She needed to free Dreamy and get the item she had put in there for her.

"Come now, Amirah, you know that it is a man's right to demand his pleasure where and how he will," Darius rasped down at her, angry that she still defied him.

"Your little uprising caused me so many problems," Darius's eyes glittered with anger. "Silver Valley is almost uncontrollable these days. It is full of clan vampires with no respect. Their kind are like vermin polluting the sacred ground of the valley." His eyes turned manic, but he reigned himself in as his lips moved closer to Amirah's, his voice now filling with desire. "You and I are going to restore the valley to its former glory and regain its power."

Darius breathed out, his breath blowing on Amirah's face, making her cringe. He continued, "You will finally honor your bondage to me and take back your essence. To give me the only pure-bred heirs." Darius's hand fingered the ruby. "You will be my queen, and eventually, the only remaining female vampire," he sneered.

"What do you mean, the only remaining female vampire?" Amirah asked, fear of her fellow vampire females growing inside her. What was this mad vampire up to?

"Vampire women are nothing but a thorn in any living creature's side," Darius spat. "They have grown to be uncontrollable and have even challenged the vampire high council's rules." He walked to the glass partition staring out at the dance floor before turning back to them with anger in his eyes. "They have even wormed their way onto the council and are running for power in the high council elections." Darius pointed at Amirah. "You, Zara, are the reason your vampire sex will become extinct. You and your rebellious ways." He looked her up and down as if she was nothing more than an ugly stain.

"How do you expect to repopulate the vampire empire without females?" Amirah felt the burn as she wiggled her hands.

"That child, your little assistant, is carrying is our future, Zara," Darius told her. "All the vampires that were born the year before the silver poisoning can still produce seed." His eyes sparkled with manic delight. "It turns out that human females are the perfect vessels for breeding any magical creature. They have the most remarkable DNA that can be manipulated to produce the perfect offspring."

Darius walked to Rachel and touched her face. "Two perfect female specimens with potent antibodies, and one male vampire." As he finished, the guards dragged in a bound Bradley. "And with this new vaccine that every woman under the age of thirty is being given around the world in the guise of an anti-cancer drug, vampires will once again reign supreme."

"Bradley," both Rachel and Sophie shouted to the

delight of Darius, who ordered the guards to take him away.

"Human females are also a lot easier to control," Darius once again leaned over Amirah.

"You are a fool, Darius, to think your plan will work," Amirah hissed as her burning fingers inched towards Sophie's purse, and she nudged Dreamy into action.

"And once we are truly bonded, we can unlock the Seat of Power, and your grandfather will have no option but to give the title to me," he yanked the necklace off her neck, finger it again, "So beautiful," he whispered.

"Bring them," Darius ordered the guards as he turned to swish out of the room only to be stopped and sprayed on by a furious dragon that clearly hated him. "Agh, get that foul beast away…"

Before he could say more, Amirah spun him around and punched Darius flying before telling Luka, "Go deal with the soldiers and help the others. I've got this."

Darius sprang to his feet; the dragon's spray had only partially gotten him on the side of his face. He clutched the Stone of Zara and held it out towards Amirah as he started chanting.

Amirah was unfazed by it and walked towards him. "Do you really think I would have brought something so powerful into a trap?" Amirah snatched the necklace and dodged his punch as he ducked around her.

They circled each other; Darius loved to play with his prey while Amirah was driven with centuries of anger and hate. "Ah, Zara, I am going to enjoy you so much tonight for this," he laughed, grabbing her as she lunged towards him. He turned her, holding her captive with her back to him and deliberately pressed himself into her, so she knew what he meant. He cupped her face by her chin and ran his cheek against hers. "I missed your skin," he whispered.

So caught up by his want for her, he spun her around. Cupping her face, he was about to take her lips with when his eyes widened, a sting burning across his throat. He let her go and fell back, holding his neck as the sticky feeling of blood bubbled from where Amirah had slit his throat.

"If I remember correctly," Amirah looked at him dead in the eye, enjoying the fear in his for a change as he fell back against the glass dome. "That is how you slaughtered my mother and then made my father watch as she suffered a horrible death, drowning in her own blood."

She watched him, her eyes burning with rage and disgust, as the gilded fob fell to his knees, gasping for breath like a fish out of water. "You nearly took everyone I loved from me. You locked my brothers and I up like slaves and tortured us over and over again." The anger, fear, and torment this man had made her suffering fueled the darkest parts of Amirah.

He had abused her repeatedly, blaming her for inciting the women of the valley to rebel against his tyranny. Then when she refused to submit, he turned his sadism onto her younger brothers. She lifted the jeweled dagger Rohan had given her and drove it into Darius's stomach. "You like my grandfather so much; you can spend eternity with him."

Darius tried to scream as the dark wrapped around him and dragged him off to the Okapi Grove.

TWENTY-TWO

Tomorrow Is Another Day

AMIRAH AND LUKA WALKED BACK TO THE VAN, STOPPING a distance away when Luka grabbed her hand, pulling her to him needing to feel her lips on his.

Amirah sighed contentedly when the kiss ended. They stood with their arms around each other. Watching the team that had now become their family pile into the van. They both knew there was still a lot to sort through and that Darius was only part of a much larger evil. The Rites of Adam spanned the globe and were now running the amalgamation of two of the world's most influential organizations. Not to mention the vaccine being distributed to women everywhere with the fate of both the female vampire and human male in peril.

They were also still fugitives and had a lot of work ahead if they were to try and stop the faction. Word had gotten to them that Matthew and Vincent, Nicholas's brother, were still alive, as was Bradley, or Bry as he was now known. They had all made a pact tonight that they would bring down these factions, no matter how deep the rot went. They would protect the innocent and find Matthew, Ty, and Nicholas.

The druids had been summoned by Rohan and were taking care of all the members of the Rites of Adam they could round up. Although they did not form alliances, they also did not tolerate those trying to tip the delicate balance of magic and nature. Rohan had told the team the druids would help them bring down the faction.

But tomorrow was another day. Tonight, they would take this victory, not just as a team but a family bonded by the grueling challenges of the past week.

"So, should we talk about you becoming one of my vampires?" she smiled at Luka, who shook his head and kissed her.

"I don't think I am the O-neg type guy. I am more the burger and fries type." He held her in the circle of his arms, smiling down at her. He could not remember ever feeling so happy or content.

"I have not seen you eating burgers and fries," she teased him, and he laughed.

"Do you know who lives with me?" They both turned and watched Sophie sitting in the van with a plate piled with food from the function that she was grudgingly sharing with Theo and Dreamy. "I have to hide my food, or I would never get to eat with Sophie around."

They both laughed before Amirah said, "But seriously, Luka, I love you and the thought of losing you ..." Her eyes searched his shining with fear and love.

Luka kissed her forehead, "I could not bear to lose you either, Amirah. But I am not the type of guy who could give you up as easily as your clan vampires did when you no longer needed them."

Amirah felt hurt at his words, but she knew them to be accurate; everyone knew her for her fickleness, but she had never felt this way before. "I would not do that to you, Luka. You are my heart and my soul." She reached into the pocket of her jacket and handed him an ancient key for which she received a questioning look from him as she whispered, "It is the key to my soul."

"I don't have a key for you, and you know I can't make promises about my mortality. But you too have my heart for as long as I live," Luka told her softly before bestowing a lingering kiss on her lips.

Getting impatient, the team yelled for them to get back to the van as they wanted to go home.

As they turned and walked to the vehicle, Amirah said to him, "We are going to have to talk to Sophie and Theo about a certain golden feather."

"Agreed," Luka said as they turned to look at Theo and Sophie sitting chatting. "But that is a problem for tomorrow," Luka said as he pulled the driver's door shut. "Right now, let's just get home."

Luka turned the van in the direction of the old hospital fortress they now called home.

More Books by Renee

The Monsters and the Morally Ambiguous

Tread carefully in a landscape where monsters walk among us, and morality is as fluid as the shapes they assume.

Tempest
Dead Wrong
Her Dark Pleasure
Secrets of the Dhampir

The Supernatural Sleuths and Arcane Artifacts

Prepare to delve into a world where the supernatural is woven into the fabric of everyday life.

My Soul to Reap
Vance and Vance
Cold Read
That's the Spirit
Magic Huntress
Relic Huntress

While You Were Reaping

The Cursed and the Powerful

Dive into stories of latent legacies and untamed powers, where characters grapple with the dangerous gifts bestowed upon them.

Gravetide

Strange Magic

Blade of the Guild

Brewing Up a Storm

Thank You..

Thank you for reading my book!

I really appreciate all of your feedback and I love to hear what you have to say. Please leave your review at your favorite retailer!